# The Case of the Deadly Ha-Ha Game

# The Case of the
# Deadly Ha-Ha Game

## John R. Erickson

Illustrations by Gerald L. Holmes

Puffin Books

PUFFIN BOOKS
Published by the Penguin Group
Penguin Putnam Books for Young Readers,
345 Hudson Street, New York, New York 10014, U.S.A.
Penguin Books Ltd,
27 Wrights Lane, London W8 5TZ, England
Penguin Books Australia Ltd, Ringwood, Victoria, Australia
Penguin Books Canada Ltd,
10 Alcorn Avenue, Toronto, Ontario, Canada M4V 3B2
Penguin Books (N.Z.) Ltd,
182-190 Wairau Road, Auckland 10, New Zealand

Penguin Books Ltd, Registered Offices:
Harmondsworth, Middlesex, England

Published simultaneously by Viking and Puffin Books, divisions
of Penguin Putnam Books for Young Readers, 2001

11 13 15 17 19 20 18 16 14 12

LIBRARY OF CONGRESS CATALOGING-IN-PUBLICATION DATA
Erickson, John R., date
The case of the deadly ha-ha game / by John R. Erickson ;
illustrations by Gerald L. Holmes.
p.   cm. — (Hank the Cowdog ; 37)
Summary: Hank the Cowdog, Head of Ranch Security, and assistant deputy
Drover engage in an epic battle with the coyotes, Rip and Snort,
as they all seek some meaty treats.
ISBN-13: 978-0-14-131048-0
[1. Dogs—Fiction. 2. Coyote—Fiction. 3. Ranch life—West (U.S.)—Fiction.
4. West (U.S.)—Fiction. 5. Humorous stories. 6. Mystery and detective stories.]
I. Holmes, Gerald L., ill. II. Title.
PZ7.E72556 Cacf 2001  [Fic]—dc21  00-062659

*This one is for our grandsons,*
*Kale Erickson and Cameron Wilson,*
*in hopes they will discover the joy*
*of language and reading.*

# CONTENTS

# I Arrest the Cat

It's me again, Hank the Cowdog. It was spring-time, as I recall, and the mystery began on a Tuesday evening. Wednesday. It doesn't matter. It happened, that's the important thing. That was the night we went out in search of the Fabled Treasure of the Potted Chicken and found ourselves involved in the Case of the Deadly Ha-Ha Game.

Yes, of course it was, and we were almost eaten by ... wait a second. This is all classified information, and I mean, very secret. Those files on the Ha-Ha Game have been sealed and aren't supposed to be viewed by anyone outside of the Security Division.

Why? Well, for one thing, it turned out to be a pretty scary case. Furthermore, if we opened the

1

files, someone might get the impression that Pete . . . I'm sorry, we can't go any further with this. Just forget I said anything about the Deadly Ha-Ha Game.

Those files are missing from our, uh, files. No kidding.

I was . . . misquoted. If anyone asks if I blurted out any secret information about the so-forths, tell 'em no, I was merely misquoted. Tell 'em I was talking about barbecued steak, not some wild and dangerous contest with the Coyote Brotherhood.

And speaking of barbecued steaks, at precisely five o'clock in the evening, I noticed something unusual. High Loper, the owner of this outfit, came home from the hay field and went inside the house. This was unusual, because at five o'clock in the evening, in the springtime in the Texas Panhandle, we still have three hours of daylight left.

Do you see what this meant? It meant that Loper had quit work before dark. Pretty strange. It wasn't his usual pattern, especially during hay season.

Drover and I were up at the machine shed, crunching tasteless kernels of Co-op dog food from the overturned Ford hubcap that served as our official dog bowl. And in case you wondered, the answer is yes—the old hubcap still held the faint taste and aroma of axle grease, so that with every bite of Co-op, we were reminded that our official dog bowl was nothing more than a piece of junk.

You'd think our human friends would have jumped at the chance to provide us with a bowl of . . . well, gold or silver, or even cast iron, but that's not the way it had turned out. We took our meals from a smelly old hubcap and tried not to think of the terrible injustice of . . . so forth.

Anyway, there we were, Drover and I, crunching Co-op dog food kernels, when I noticed the business about Loper quitting work in the middle of the day. Okay, it wasn't exactly the middle of the day, but I found it pretty unusual that Loper would be quitting work at five o'clock in the evening.

"What do you think, Drover? Pretty strange, huh?"

"Yeah, it reminds me of stale grease. And I think it's made out of sawdust."

I stopped chewing and stared at him. "The hay baler is made out of sawdust?"

"No, I'm talking about our dog food."

"Why are you talking about our dog food?"

"I don't know. 'Cause that's what I'm eating, I guess."

"It's not polite to talk while you're eating,

Drover. You should never chew with your mouth full."

"Yeah, but you can't chew when your mouth's empty, 'cause when your mouth's empty, there's nothing to chew."

"Don't argue with me. You should never chew with your . . . did I say that you should never *chew* with your mouth full? What I meant to say was that you should never *talk* with your mouth full." I took a bite of Co-op. "Does that sound better?"

"You mean the way you crunched the dog food?"

"No, I mean . . . never mind, Drover. The point is that you should never talk with your mouth full."

"Yeah, but that's what you're doing right now. I know, 'cause you just spit a crumb on me."

"See? That's my whole point. When you try to talk with your mouth stuffed, you end up spewing crumbs all over the party to who or whom you're speaking."

"Yeah, and there's another crumb."

"So let this be a lesson to you. Never chew with your mouth full."

"I think I've got it now."

"Good. Now, I was trying to call your attention to a very interesting detail: Loper just went into the house and it's only five o'clock."

He gave me a troubled look. "The house is only five o'clock?"

"No, the house is where he lives."

"Oh. That's what I thought but . . ."

"The clock says five."

He glanced around. "Where's the clock?"

"The clock is . . . it doesn't matter where the clock is, Drover. Any clock would say that it's five o'clock, because it *is* five o'clock."

"How does a clock know what time it is?"

"That's what clocks do, Drover. They tell time."

"What do they tell it?"

"They tell it that it's five o'clock."

"But wouldn't time already know what time it was? Why does it need a clock?"

"It needs a clock because . . . are you trying to make this complicated? I made the simple statement that it's five o'clock. Do you believe that or not?"

"Well . . ." He rolled his eyes around. "What about yesterday? Wasn't it five o'clock yesterday?"

I stuck my nose in his face and lifted my lips into a snarl. "Drover, sometimes I feel that you're trying to make a mockery of my life's work. And furthermore, we're out of time for your foolish questions."

"Well, it's about time."

"Exactly my point. Now, I'm going down to the yard to investigate."

"What did it do?"

"What?"

"The gate. What did the gate do?"

"I don't know what you're talking about."

"Well, you said you were going down to arrest the gate."

My eyes began to bulge and I felt my temper rising. "I said that I was going down to the yard gate to *investigate*. IN-VES-TI-GATE. Do you stay awake at night, thinking of ways to bring chaos into our conversations? Or does it happen naturally?"

"Oh, I guess it just happens. Did you notice that Loper came back to the house, and it's only five o'clock?"

I stared into the huge vacuum of his eyes. "Drover, I pointed that out ten minutes ago, and then you . . . never mind. I'm leaving. I'm getting out of here, and don't ever speak to me again."

And with that, I left the little lunatic and marched down to arrest the gate.

Investigate.

See what he does to me?

By the time I reached the yard gate, I had managed to clear most of the toxic fumes that Drover had released into my brainial cavity. And upon reaching the gate, I activated all my sensory equipment and began gathering clues.

Clue #1: Loper had gone inside the house.

Clue #2: The yard appeared to be empty.

Clue #3: What we had here was . . . well, no clues, no case, and nothing of any particular interest . . . except . . .

Aha! A cat. Yes, we had a cat in the yard, on the other side of the fence. Right away, I picked him up on VizRad (Visual Radar) and ran his profile through Data Control. Within seconds, the report came back, and it confirmed my initial impression.

It was Pete the Barncat. Mister Never Sweat. Mister Kitty Moocher. He was lying in the iris patch on the north side of the house, lounging in the shade and staring at me with his big cattish eyes. Oh, and his tail was sticking straight up and flicking back and forth. That seemed pretty suspicious.

Right away, I punched in Sirens and Lights and reached for the microphone of my mind. "Okay, Kitty, we see you there," I called out. "Come out with your tail up. We'll need to check some identification."

He came, but took his sweet time. He pushed

himself up from the iris patch, threw a curve into his back, and stretched all four legs. Oh, and he yawned. I picked that up right away, and even got a count on his spiky little teeth (seven). I'm sure the cat had no idea that he was being observed, photographed, mapped, and memorized, but he was. It all went straight to Data Control.

He came slithering out into the fading sunlight and slithered his way over to the gate—again, taking his sweet time. This was a typical cat trick, and we'd seen it before. He used it as a provocatory gesture, don't you see, because he knew that I hate to wait. I hate to wait for anyone or anything, but I especially hate to wait for a cat.

Have we discussed my Position on Cats? I don't like 'em, never have. I'm against all cats but especially Pete. He's a troublemaker, and he also causes trouble.

And here he came, slithering and grinning. I watched him with daggerish eyes. I could feel my lips quivering and trying to rise into a snarl. "Hurry up, cat, we don't have all day."

"I'm coming, Hankie, I'm coming."

You know what he did? *He slowed down.* Yes sir, I saw him. He probably thought this would provoke me into a burst of angry barking that would draw the attention of Sally May and get

me in trouble. Ha. Little did he know that I had been to school on cats and had learned to control my savage instinks.

No, I washed and watted. I watted and wayched. *I waited and watched,* shall we say, and tried to get a firm grip on my lip, and okay, it wasn't so easy—standing there, waiting for a sniveling little cat whilst my whole inner bean was trembling and aching with a desire to snarl and bark and give him a pounding.

But I managed to control myself. Everything but my upper lip, which continued to twitch. "Okay, let's see some ID, Pete. State your name, rank, and cereal, and be quick about it."

And so the mystery began.

# CHAPTER TWO

# Secret Files
# on Slim

He grinned at me through the fence between us—Pete did. "Well, Hankie, if you already know my name, why do I need to say it?"

"We don't make up the rules, Kitty, we just follow orders. Skip the name and go on to rank. What's your rank?"

"My rank." He licked his left front paw. "Let me think, Hankie. I guess I'd have to call myself," he blinked his eyes, "King of the Ranch. How does that sound?"

I wasn't amused. "Okay, pal, have it your way. Drover, get the cuffs on him. Drover?" I whirled around. Drover wasn't there. He was still up at the machine shed—watching us. "Drover, I'm calling for backup. Get yourself down here at once."

He came ambling down the hill. "Will you hurry? We need to get the caffs on this cup."

He finally got there and gave me a frown. "Where's the cup?"

"I know nothing about a cup, Drover, nor do I want to discuss cups."

"Yeah, but you said to get the caffs on the cup. I heard it with my own ears."

Pete nodded and grinned. "That's what you said, Hankie. I heard it too."

My steely gaze flicked from one face to the other. "Is this some kind of trick? Drover, you've been given a direct order. *Get the cuffs on this cat.*"

His eyes popped open. "Yeah, but . . . he's on the other side of the fence."

"Right. Jump the fence."

"Yeah, but . . . then I'd be in Sally May's yard."

"Right. It's a risk we'll have to take. Move."

"Yeah, but . . . what if Pete scratches me with his claws?"

"You're authorized to use lethal force, Drover. Quit stalling."

"Well, I'd really like to, Hank, but you know, this old leg . . ."

"Are you refusing to obey an order? Is that what you're saying?"

"Well, I wouldn't want to put it that way, but

12

boy, this old leg just went out on me, and I'm not sure . . . "

"Okay, Drover, skip the cuffs. Never mind. I'll handle this without a backup, but I'm warning you. Every word of this will go into my report."

"Oh darn."

"Including your use of naughty language on the job."

"Oh fiddle."

"Go ahead, pile 'em on, son, get 'em out of your system."

"Oh drat. Oh phooey. Oh woosle."

"Woosle's not a word."

"Oh figgleblossom. Oh wigglesnort."

"Hold it, stop, halt. That's enough to send you to the brig for twenty years." I whirled around to the cat. "Okay, Kitty, we'll skip the cuffs this time. Tell me about your cereal."

"Well, let me see here." The cat blinked his eyes several times. "My favorite is Kitty Yums."

"Kitty Yums, okay, got it. Is that all?"

"Well, sometimes Sally May gives me Yummy Cat, and it's pretty good too. I'll bet you dogs would love it."

"Ha. Not likely. We have our own rations, Kitty, and it's great stuff."

"I know, Hankie, I've tasted it. It's the special

Sawdust-and-Grease flavor, isn't it?"

I narrowed my eyes. "Okay, Pete, maybe it's not so great. What's your point?"

He rolled over on his back and began rubbing the . . . I don't know what. The ground, I suppose, and he was still grinning. That put me on the alert. A grinning cat is up to no good. "Well, I just thought you dogs might want to try some of my . . . Yummy Cat."

I laughed in his face and turned to my assistant. "Did you hear that, Drover? He thinks we might . . ." I whirled back to the cat. "What flavor is this . . . this so-called Yummy Cat?"

"Well, let's see, Hankie. Sometimes it's strawberry and sometimes it's chocolate and sometimes it's fish and sometimes it's liver. But my favorite is . . . steak flavor."

HUH?

My ears shot up, more or less on their own. I mean, there was something about the word *steak* that, well, got my full attention and caused my mouth to . . . uh . . . water. I swept my tongue across my lips to conceal the evidence, and moved closer to the cat.

"Did you say . . . steak? Is that what you said?"

"Uh-huh. Do you like steak, Hankie?"

Before I could answer the question, the back

door opened and Loper came out into the yard. He was wearing the silliest costume I'd ever seen him wear: shorts that exposed his skinny white legs, a T-shirt, sandals, and a baseball cap.

I stared at him in disbelief. *Was this a cowboy? Wearing such clothes? I could hardly believe my . . .* okay, I began following the trail of clues and realized that he had quit work early that afternoon and had come home to cook dinner out on the barbecue grill.

Yes, of course. It was all coming clear now. These were his Outdoor Barbecue Clothes.

He walked over to the barbecue grill, and appeared to be carrying a plate of something in his right hand. Left hand. Who cares? He was carrying a plate and set it down on the little tray on the side of the grill. Then he lifted the lid, threw some small chunks of mesquite wood inside, and squirted the wood with . . . what did he call it?

Boy Scout Juice. Yes, that was it, Boy Scout Juice. And then he lit a match and flipped it onto the wood, and it began to burn. That was a pretty neat trick, catching a load of mesquite on fire with one match. I mean, mesquite is hard wood and hard to catch on fire, right? But Loper did it with one match. Pretty amazing, although . . .

Okay, I soon realized that the so-called Boy Scout Juice was actually *charcoal lighter,* and that Loper was using shortcuts and tricks to get his fire started. But in typical cowboy fashion, he had invented a phony name for it, to conceal the fact that . . . I don't know what.

Maybe he was trying to be funny. They do that all the time, you know, and we dogs have a terrible time trying to figure out what's going on. I mean, what's wrong with calling charcoal lighter *charcoal lighter*? Call it what it is and then everyone, including us dogs, will know what we're talking about.

But that's not what they do. They make up all these silly names and they're always trying to be funny, but they're not. Not funny at all. If you ask me . . . never mind.

Anyway, the record will show that Loper was a lazy fire-builder and used dangerous explosives to start his mesquite fire. He looked into the fire for a few minutes, then glanced at his watch and said, "Twenty minutes." And then he and his skinny, ridiculous, mayonnaise-colored legs went back into the house.

Let me tell you, if I owned a pair of legs like that, I would keep them covered up. I would undress in a darkened room, maybe even a cellar, and I would never expose them to the general public, not even to my loyal dogs.

But you know, one of the more touching aspects of our relationship with humans is that we dogs keep many dark secrets about our masters. It's part of our Cowdog Oath. We are sworn never to reveal the dark secrets of their lives.

Take Slim Chance for example. The general public sees him as a normal man, your average hired hand on your average cattle ranch. Only his dogs know the truth, the awful truth, and it's so shocking that I'm not at liberty to reveal it.

Honest, no kidding. I've sworn a solemn oath

and I sure wouldn't want to . . . I mean, this kind of stuff is supposed to remain sealed for fifty or sixty years.

But what the heck, maybe it wouldn't hurt . . .

If I revealed several of the darkest truths about Slim, would you promise never to repeat them? I mean, a dog could get himself into a world of trouble if this ever leaked out.

Tell you what. I'll let you peek at a secret report about Slim, things known only to his loyal dogs, but you must forget that you ever saw them. Promise? Okay, here we go. Hang on.

## Shocking Revelations File #425-33309-47576B
## For Dogs Only: Top Secret

**Shocking Revelation #1:** The elastic in Slim's undershorts is so old and worn out, he has trouble keeping them up. They slip down, in other words, and one of these days they're liable to end up around his ankles.

**Shocking Revelation #2:** Slim doesn't change his socks every day. That is one reason his boots stink. The other reason is that his boots are ten years old.

**Shocking Revelation #3:** When he does change socks, he chooses socks with holes in them.

Some have a hole at the toe, others are worn through at the heel. His reason for continuing to wear them is—this is a direct quote from Slim—"the holes are at the ends and the rest of the sock is still in good shape."

**Shocking Revelation #4:** Slim snores in his sleep. He denies this, but if you want the truth, ask his dogs. Believe me, he snores, and two winters ago, he snored so loud he cracked a window in his bedroom. No kidding.

### End of Top Secret File

So there we are, the whole book on Slim's darkest secrets. There may be others, but this will do for now. At this point, you should forget you ever read this stuff. You promised.

But we were talking about Loper, weren't we? Yes. He had just started his mesquite fire in the barbecue grill and had gone back inside the house with his ridiculous pale legs, leaving me and Drover to finish our heartless interrogation of the . . .

*Sniff, sniff.*

. . . of the cat, the dumb cat. Suddenly I caught the scent of something good riding around on the evening breeze. *Sniff, sniff.* And the smell bore a faint resemblance to the aroma of . . . well, fresh steak.

I whirled around to the cat. "Back to work, Kitty. You had just told this court about your favorite brand of cat food, something called Yummy Tummy."

"Yummy Cat, Hankie."

"Whatever. And you had told this court that your favorite flavor was . . . what?"

"Let me think. Strawberry?"

"No. Forget the strawberry. We have no use for berries. Get to the point."

He fluttered his eyelids. "Let's see, Hankie. Was it . . . chocolate?"

I pushed my nose into his face and curled my lips. "Out with it, Kitty, you know what we're looking for. Steak. That's what you said, and don't try to deny it."

"I said steak?"

"Right. You said steak. And since you've already said it, you can't take it back. You told this court that your Yummy Tummy comes in steak flavor. You also hinted that if we dogs wished to run some tests on this variety of Yummy Tummy . . ."

"Yummy Cat, Hankie."

". . . you would have no objections. Isn't that what you told this court? Tell the truth, Pete. For once in your life, face the truth and be brave. I know that telling the truth is hard on you cats, but in the long run, it's the best course."

"Well . . . since you put it that way, Hankie, all right. That's what I said. Yes."

"Thank you, Pete. No further questions." I gave the witness a worldly sneer. I had broken him down with relentless drill-bit questions, and had finally emerged with The Truth.

CHAPTER THREE

# The Mystery of the Yummy Tummy

"And now, Kitty, I will enter the yard and take this investigation to the next level. According to our sources, I have exactly twenty minutes to conduct a thorough Search and Test. You're excused, Kitty. Thank you, good-bye, and go chase your tail."

*Sniff, sniff.*

Yes, it was steak, no question about it. Or to bring it more in line with the, uh, investigation in progress, we had every reason to suppose that the mysterious aroma was coming from Pete's bowl of . . . well, steak-flavored Yummy Tummy.

Yummy Cat.

I mean, he'd revealed the information about the steak-flavored Yummy Tummy before we'd ever gotten a whiff of it, right? Hence, following the trail of simple logic, we had every reason to believe that the smells and aromas riding the evening breeze had come from Pete's cat food. Any dog trained in Security Work would have arrived at that conclusion.

And since we had obtained a warrant to search the yard and to sample Pete's cat food, the next step in the investigation was for me to . . . well, do a quick Yard Entry and check this thing out.

I rolled the muscles in my enormous shoulders and warmed up the huge Jumpus Muscles in my hind legs. "You'd better move, Kitty. Once we launch this thing, we have no control over where it lands."

The cat didn't move, heh heh, which was just fine. I took a deep breath of air, went into a deep crouch situation, and hit the Bonzai Launch button. Smoke, flames, and a loud roar filled the air, and I went flying over the fence. And darn the luck, landed right on top of Kitty-Kitty.

Heh heh.

"Oops, sorry Pete, I tried to warn you. Get out of the way."

He hissed and growled and moved his freight a few steps away. Oh, and I noticed that he was beaming dark glares in my direction, but at that

point I didn't care what he did, because we had just done a clean penetration into Sally May's precious yard.

Once on the ground, we went straight into Infrared Scanners and activated Smelloradar. Information streamed into Data Control, and it brought a real surprise. See, before the launch, we had assumed that the, uh, waves of steakness had been coming from Kitty's bowl near the back porch. But now, as we analyzed the sniffatory data, we came up with a startling revelation.

The waves of steakness seemed to be coming from *the plate Loper had left on the barbecue grill.*

Do you see the meaning of this? I was shocked. Stunned. For you see, it meant that Loper was planning to barbecue a plateload of steak-flavored Yummy Tummy cat food for supper!

Why would he do such a thing? We didn't know, had no idea. Maybe they were out of beef at the house. Maybe Loper was too stingy to fix real steak for his family. I mean, that fit, didn't it? This was the same guy who expected the elite forces of the Security Division to eat out of a greasy hubcap, right? The same guy who was too tight with his money to build the Security Division the kind of huge office complex we deserved, right?

Well, this sent the case charging into an entirely

new direction. See, we had already obtained a search warrant for Pete's cat food, and . . . do you see where this is leading?

It meant that we were authorized by a court of law to search out and test a secret stash of Yummy Tummy cat food in the yard, and we now had irreguffable proof that Loper's plate contained steak-flavored Yummy Tummy.

Pretty amazing, huh? You bet it was, and I can tell you that all of us in the search party felt a little . . . well, uneasy about following this astounding new lead in the case. It meant that we would have to take our samples, so to speak, from Loper's plate, and this threw the case into a High Risk Situation. If we were caught with our noses in the plate . . . well, it could be very bad and very dangerous.

I narrowed my eyes and did a complete 360-degree sweep of the immediate vicinity. Drover was watching from the other side of the fence. Pete was staring at me with his big, cunning eyes and flicking the end of his tail back and forth. But the important thing was that our, uh, friends in the house were . . . well, in the house, which meant that . . .

*Sniff, sniff.*

. . . which meant that we had a job to do, an

important job. We'd been trained for it and there was no turning back now. We took one last reading of our location and punched in the numbers for our final approach.

Would you care to take a peek at those numbers? I guess it wouldn't hurt. The numbers, in the order of their entry into the system, were 323, 12, 90, and 3. Pretty impressive, huh? You bet, and those were all real numbers, not some kind of decoy numbers.

Well, having done all the so-forth, I began creeping toward the barbecue cooker on paws that made not a sound. Ten feet. Eight feet. Six feet. Four feet. (Those are distance figures, by the way, not the number of feet or paws on my body.)

Three feet away from the target, I heard a whiny voice behind me. It said, and this is a direct quote, it said, "Hankie, the cat bowl is over by the porch."

That was Pete, of course, and for a moment I was gripped by a sudden impulse to laugh, but I resisted. Instead, I turned my head and replied in a low voice, "Never mind, Kitty. We've just received some information that is going to blow this case wide open."

And then I returned to Stealthy Crouch Mode and resumed my relentless pursuit of the truth. I had to know. Was Loper actually feeding cat food to his family?

Two feet. One foot. By this time I could feel the heat, the terrible heat of the roaring fire in the cooker. Many dogs would have quit right there, shut 'er down and aborted the mission because of the high danger factor. Not me, fellers. The searing heat merely sniffened my resolve to follow this thing to a conclusion . . . *stiffened* my resolve, shall we say, no matter where it led, no matter whose life was scorched by the Fire of Truth.

Yes, the steaks were high. The *stakes,* that is. High stakes.

I stopped and made one last visual sweep of the yard. Then, without a sound, I went to Hydraulic Lift on the back legs and raised myself to the level of the . . . uh . . . plate.

*Sniff, sniff.*

WOW!

And at that point, I made another amazing discovery. You won't believe this. See, you probably thought we would find (1) a plate full of Yummy Tummy Kitty bits or (2) a plate full of T-bone steaks. Isn't that what you thought? Go ahead and admit it.

Well, you were wrong, and you'd better hang on for this. Even I was surprised, nay, shocked, by the

discovery that awaited me when my eyes fell upon the contents of the plate.

It didn't contain mere Kitty food, and it wasn't loaded with a huge stack of fresh, luscious T-bone steaks.

Make a guess. I dare you.

No.

No, that's wrong, too.

Nope, not that either.

No, sorry, you had three guesses and you missed. If you'd had a hundred guesses, you still would have missed.

Chicken? No.

Sausage? Not even close.

Ribs? No, and we're out of time for guessing.

Here's the answer, which you will find shocking and hard to believe.

The plate was piled high with Yummy Tummy cat food, just as we had suspected, but *it had been molded into the shape of T-bone steaks*!

This was an amazing discovery.

I mean, those counterfeit steaks looked so real, most dogs would have been fooled. And they not only looked real, but they smelled real. No kidding. They smelled exactly like real genuine steaks, and your ordinary dogs would have fallen for the trick—hook, line, and sewer.

Ordinary dogs would have backed away and left the yard, thinking that those fraudulent cat food T-bones were the genuine article, and therefore off-limits to all dogs. But I saw through all the tricks and disguises, and knew, in my deepest heart of hearts, that those so-called steaks were just a shabby imitation of the . . .

*Sniff, sniff.*

. . . a pretty good shabby imitation of the real thing, but an imitation nonetheless. They were nothing but cat food, molded and shaped into a near-perfect counterfeit of real steaks, and since I had been authorized to sample and test Pete's cat food, I had no choice but to . . . uh . . . proceed with the . . . uh . . . procedure.

Operating now on nothing but cunning and superior intelligence, I fitted my enormous jaws around one of the st . . . around one of the, uh, counterfeit meat products, shall we say, and lifted it off the plate. I hit the Down Button and let the Hydraulic Legs Mechanism ease me back to earth. Cutting my eyes from side to side, I turned and made a dash for the fence.

Another shocking discovery awaited me. There was little Drover, staring at me with wild, greedy eyes. "Oh boy, a steak! I get bites!"

With my mouth filled with st . . . with counterfeit meat products, I said, "This isn't a steak, Drover," only it came out as, "Miff miffn't a mafe, Mofer."

And at that very same moment, I caught a flash of movement out of the right corner of my periphery. It was Pete, Mister Kitty Moocher, and he too was staring at me with big greedy eyes.

"Well, Hankie, I think I'd like bites too."

To which I growled, "Get away from my treasure, Kitty," only it came out as, "Mitt amay fumm mah measure, Mitty." Or something like that.

Do you think the greedy little creep took the hint? Oh no. I'd done all the work, taken all the risks, made a flawless penetration into the yard, and had captured a specimen of st . . . of phony

31

cat food meat products, and now Pete wanted to share the loot.

Ha. How foolish of the cat. Did he think I would just stand there and let him drool and slobber all over my st . . . all over my evidentiary piece of counterfeit so-forth? Heck no! I dropped the, uh, specimen and went to Tiger Teeth and Savage Glares.

But at that very moment . . . I couldn't believe this, you won't believe it either . . . Drover leaped over the fence, snatched up my court-appointed evidence, and ran off with it! Drover did that! Drover, the same guy who'd been moaning and crying about his bad leg, remember?

Well, you know me. Would I just stand there and allow the runt to steal important court-appointed evidence? No sir. I went straight into Turbo Four and caught the little thief just as he was nearing the northwest corner of the house. I rolled him and snatched the precious evidentiary material from his thieving jaws and . . . huh?

Pete was right there, waiting like the little glutton, the little moocher he truly was. Before I knew it, he had latched onto the st . . . the specimen, and suddenly we found ourselves engaged in a deadly game of tug-of-war. He pulled south and I pulled north. He had turned on that police siren yowl of his and his ears were pinned down on his head.

Me? I tugged with all my might and snarled a warning. "Miff muff muffin murkle, Mitty!"

Pretty scary, huh? Well, it got even worse.

# CHAPTER FOUR

# Pete's Slip
# of the Tongue

**D**rover, little Mister Buttinski, jumped up and took a bite on the northwest corner of the st . . . of my evidence. Now we had a tug-of-war going in three different directions. But just then . . .

Oops.

The back door flew open. We froze, all three of us, froze like . . . something. Like frozen statues of frozen ice in the freezing frozenness. Someone came out the door.

Gulp.

Did I dare abandon my treasure and run? That would have been a sensible thing to do because, let's face it, the person who had just emerged from the house might very well be . . . Sally May.

Remember her? Sally May of the deadly broom.

Sally May of the Thermonuclear Moments. Sally May who didn't allow dogs in her yard, and who had shown some indications that she . . . well, I had reason to believe she just didn't like me.

It was a tense moment. I heard footsteps. My heart almost stopped beating. I rolled my eyes around and saw . . .

WHEW!

It wasn't Sally May, as you might have supposed, but Little Alfred, her five-year-old son—and also a great pal of mine. I knew he would understand about the counterfeit Yummy Tummy steaks. The boy and I had been through many dark moments and harrowing experiences, and we'd built up a great relationship based on trust.

In his deepest heart, Little Alfred knew that I wasn't the kind of dog who would . . . well, steal a steak in broad daylight. He would never believe such a pack of lies and gossip about his beloved . . .

He saw us, Alfred did. His jaw dropped open and his eyes widened. And then he let out a gaps and said, "Uh-oh! Y'all got into my dad's steaks!"

Gasp. He let out a gasp, not a gaps.

Okay, what we had here was a situation that had gotten out of control. It appeared that my pal Alfred had fallen for the obvious, and suddenly it occurred to me that I would never be able to

explain all the ins and outs of this case—that I had entered the yard to test Pete's cat food, that Loper's steaks had turned out to be made of . . .

No, it was too complicated to explain through tail wags and facial expressions and our other forms of communication media. Sometimes life goes beyond our ability to explain it, don't you see, and when that happens . . .

But the good news was that Pete and Drover were there to, uh, share the blame, so to speak, and all at once I saw the light at the end of the turnip. Here's what I did. You'll be impressed.

I released my grip on the steak, and in a very mature manner, walked away from the scene of greed and shameless behavior. I marched straight over to Alfred, sat down at his feet, and went into a program that we call "I Didn't Do It, Honest."

This is a difficult program. It requires Slow Sweeps on the tail section and eyes that express . . . well, great sadness and disappointment that my companions had done this terrible thing. Throwing all communication gear into the effort, I beamed Alfred looks that said:

"Alfred, I know this looks bad, but let me explain. You see, I happened to be passing the yard when I noticed that Drover and Pete had conspired to steal one of your daddy's, uh, steaks. Naturally,

I was shocked and outraged, and without thinking . . . I mean, I was driven by a higher sense of
duty . . . without thinking, I rushed to the scene of
the crime, and when you walked out the door, I was
in the process of, uh, trying to return the steak to
its rightful owner. No kidding."

I ran the entire program and then studied the
boy's face to see if he was buying it. He looked at
me. He glanced over at Pete and Drover, who were
still tugging at the steak. Then he looked at me
again, just as I poured Extra Sincerity into my
presentation of wags and looks.

I had a feeling this was going to work. Yes,
because all at once he stormed over to the villains.
He booted Pete away and snatched the steak out
of Drover's jaws. "No no! You can't have this steak,
you naughty dog. This is our supper."

Drover wilted on hearing those terrible words,
"naughty dog." He cringed, cowered, and groveled
his way to the fence, hopped out of the yard, and
ran away, weeping—a dog who had been exposed
and shamed for all the world to see.

I bounded over and took my place at Alfred's
side. While he picked grass and dirt specks off
the steak, I turned a look of righteous anger at
the cat. "Pete, I can't believe you would stoop
so low—stealing food from your own family! I'm

shocked. How much lower can you sink?"

His ears lay flat on his head and he threw a hump into his back. Oh, and he hissed at me. "Very funny, Hankie, but you'll never get away with this."

"Ha! I already did, Kitty. You were nabbed with the goods, caught in the act, and now the whole world knows what a little sneak you are. And just to show you how outraged I am about this business . . ."

Heh heh. I put my nose down to his face and gave him a bark we call Full Air Horns. Heh heh. It just blew him away, the little hickocrip, rolled him up in to a ball and blew him away. Okay, maybe he managed to land one lucky punch before he was blown away . . . several lucky punches . . . he did a pretty good job of shredding my nose, shall we say, but I chased him around the north side of the house and ran him up a hackberry tree.

Gazing up at him with watering eyes, I delivered one last burst of righteous barking. "There, you little creep, and let that be a lesson to you! Next time you feel an urge to steal from your friends, don't forget that cheaters never weep and chinners never win!"

Then, holding my head at a proud angle, I whirled around and marched away. Behind me, I heard Pete say, "My goodness, there's a rainbow!"

I stopped. Rainbow? Was that some kind of

insult? Or was it a code word? I turned and marched back to the tree. "What did you just say? Something about a rainbow?"

He grinned down at me. "Oh no, Hankie. I never would have said that, because then you would try to beat me to the treasure. Oops." *He slapped a paw over his mouth.*

Hmmm. Did you notice that clue? He slapped his paw over his mouth. Obviously, this cat was trying to hide something from me. "What are you talking about?"

"Me? Oh, nothing, Hankie, nothing at all. You probably think there's a pot of gold at the end of a rainbow, but there's not. Really."

It was then that my keen eyes caught sight of a . . . well, a rainbow off to the northwest. By this time my mind was racing. Wasn't there some old superstition about rainbows? What was it?

In the blink of an eye, I did a search of Data Control's huge library of files and came up with a very interesting piece of information. Very interesting. Here, check this out.

*At the end of every rainbow, there's a pot of . . . something. Treasure.*

I could hardly conceal my delight. What a dumb cat! In a moment of weakness, he had blurted out a priceless bit of information—and he didn't even know it! He thought he'd fooled me, see, thought I hadn't noticed, hadn't caught his slip of the tongue. The foolish cat. Very little escapes my notice. Pete should have known, after all the years we'd spent matching wits, but if he didn't know it, that was fine with me.

I decided to play along with him. "Never mind, Kitty. I didn't hear you say anything about rainbows or treasures, and even if I had, I wouldn't believe it. See you around, Pete. Oh, and have a great evening up there in the tree."

And with that, I whirled and marched away, leaving Kitty Moocher sitting in the ramble of his own rubble. He didn't see the cunning smile that had formed upon my mouth, nor did he suspect that I had every intention of beating him to the potted treasure.

Basking in the glory of my huge victory over the cat, I marched back to Little Alfred. He was still picking grass and other bits of rubbish off the steak. He gazed at my nose and laughed. "Boy, Pete sure scwatched your nose."

Yes, and it grieved me to see him laughing about it. I had taken a few blows, but that had been a small price to pay, and I would wear my scars with . . .

At that point I, uh, turned my eyes toward

the . . . well, toward the steak in his hands. I mean, now that we had solved the case and brought justice to the yard, maybe he could . . . I mean, the villains had dragged the steak through the grass and surely he wasn't thinking about . . .

I moved my front paws up and down and ran my tongue over my lips. Hey, the steak was ruined, right? No longer fit for human consumation? And if he wanted to present me with a little, well, reward for heroism in the line of duty . . .

He glanced around toward the house and whispered, "Shhh. I'll put it back on the pwate and my dad'll never know. Then nobody'll get in twouble."

Twouble? Well, yes, that was something to consider, all right, and even though it broke my heart to see my reward going back to the plate . . . oh well. Easy come, easy go.

But all was not lost. At that very moment, I caught sight of Pete's cat food bowl sitting beside the porch, and proceeded to sample the, uh, merchandise.

Huh? Greasy phony steak flavor? It was awful stuff and I couldn't imagine how Pete could eat such garbage. Yuck! But it was Pete's food and so I proceeded to wolf down every bite of it—even mopped the bowl with my tongue. Tee hee. At least the cat wouldn't get it.

Don't ever eat cat food. It's so bad, cats deserve it.

At that very moment, I heard Loper coming out the back door, and I dived over the fence. When Loper reached the barbecue cooker, Alfred was rocking up and down on his toes, looking up at the clouds, and whistling, while I sat on the dog-side of the fence and beamed Looks of Perfect Innocence in all directions.

Loper was suspicious at first, and studied both of us with narrowed eyes. "What's going on around here?"

Alfred smiled and said, "Oh nuffin.' Just waiting for supper."

Loper grunted and went on with his business. He spread out the mesquite coals and placed the grill over them. Then he forked a steak and . . . uh oh . . . held it up for a closer inspection.

"How in the world did this steak get grass on it?" He looked at Alfred, who shrugged his shoulders and increased the volume of his whistling. "Huh. Wind must have done it." He slapped the steak on the grill, and then threw the others on.

Whew! Alfred and I exchanged winks and grins. We had dodged a major bullet . . . although I must say that dodging Loper's bullets wasn't all that difficult. Now, if Sally May had been in charge of the steaks, we would have had a problem. A BIG problem. She saw everything, heard everything. She was suspicious of all dogs and little boys, and we even had reason to believe that she had Radar for Naughty Thoughts.

Oh, one more item. About those counterfeit steaks, the ones made out of cat food? Nothing to it. We must have gotten some faulty readings on our instruments and, well, it was just one of those mistakes that happen in the line of, uh, duty.

A little humor there. Get it? Mistakes. Missed steaks. Ha, ha.

Anyway, Loper wasn't feeding cat food to his family after all. That was a relief. I thought you'd want to know.

Ten minutes later, Loper removed the steaks from the grill and looked off to the northwest at a puffy thunderhead cloud. "It looks a little stormy over there. I'll bet they're getting a rain up around Guymon. We could use some moisture, but I wish it would wait one more day, until I get the rest of that alfalfa baled up."

Loper and Alfred went into the house to enjoy their steak supper. I may have been rooked out of a steak, but I had something even better. *I knew about the potted treasure.*

# CHAPTER FIVE

# We Go After the Fabled Treasure

When Loper and Little Alfred went inside the house, I made my way down the hill and to the Security Division's vast office complex. I punched in the entry code on the door and took the elevator up to the . . . okay, we didn't have an elevator, and our "office complex" consisted of a couple of ragged gunnysacks beneath the gas tanks.

Might as well admit the truth.

It was a shabby place to house the entire Security Division, but that was the kind of cheapjohn outfit I worked for. You'd think the cowboys would have . . . skip it. We don't want to get started on that subject.

Anyway, I took the elevator up to the twelfth floor and entered the office, glanced at a stack of reports on my desk and checked for messages. An odd sound reached my ears, and it was then that I noticed Drover. He had crawled beneath his gunnysack and appeared to be . . . moaning.

I flopped down in my chair. "Okay, Drover, out with it. What's the problem?"

One corner of his gunnysack rose and I saw one big round eye peeking out. "What makes you think I've got a problem?"

"Because you're hiding under your bed."

"Oh, you noticed."

"Of course I noticed. And furthermore, I happen to know that when you hide under your bed, you're usually fleeing from Reality as It Really Is. So, out with it, let's get it over with."

He poked his nose out. "Well, okay. I have a broken heart."

"Broken heart. Go on. What seems to be the problem?"

"Well, I got caught with the steak and Little Alfred thought I stole it, and he . . . he called me a naughty dog!" With that, he broke into tears and boo-hoos. "It just breaks my heart!"

I gave the runt a moment to get control of himself. "Well, what can I say? You had the steak in your mouth and you got caught. You're old enough to start accepting the consequences of your own actions."

"Yeah, but it was *your* action. You stole the steak and I was just . . ."

"Hold it, stop right there, halt. I've already spotted a hole in your ointment. You said *I* stole the steak."

"Yeah, 'cause you did. I saw it myself."

"Drover, I didn't steal the steak. I had merely gathered evidence for an investigation, and that evidence just happened to be a steak."

"Yeah, but you were going to eat it. And when I saw that you were about to eat it, I wanted to eat it too, and I just couldn't control myself, and . . ." He broke down crying again. "And I got caught and now I'm a naughty dog!"

This was very sad, but I tried to hide my emotions. "I guess there's an important lesson here, son. When we fail to control our lower impulses, we get ourselves into trouble. Haven't I warned you about that? We must learn to say no to the voice of temptation."

"Yeah, but you stole the steak off the plate and I got blamed! It's not fair! All my life, I've wanted to be a good dog."

"I know you have, but Drover, you must face the fact that life is often unfair. The important thing here is that life was unfair to *you*, thus sparing me a lot of shame and embarrassment. Isn't that worth something? I mean, think about my position on this ranch. How would it look if the Head of Ranch Security got nailed for stealing a steak?"

He wiped a tear out of his eye. "Well, it would look like the truth."

"Exactly, and the truth is very important, but there are different shades of truth. The very best kind of truth is the kind that doesn't cast dark shadows on the reputations of our leaders. It was very brave of you to defend the right kind of truth."

"It was? You really think so?"

"Oh yes, no question about it. Very brave. And I wouldn't be surprised if this brought you a little promotion."

His face burst into a smile and he crawled out from under his bed. "No fooling? A promotion for me?"

"Yes sir, a nice little promotion for bravery in the face of truth."

"Oh goodie! I wonder what it might be."

I studied the claws on my right front foot. "All these years you've held the title of First Assistant Deputy Assistant, right?"

"Gosh, I didn't even know I had a title."

"You did, but now with this act of heroism in your file, we just might bump you up to the next level. How would you like to be . . . First *and* Second Assistant Deputy Assistant?"

"Really? No fooling? Gosh, I'm so proud!"

"Congratulations, soldier, you earned it."

He was hopping for joy, the little . . . He was hopping around and being joyful. "Oh, I'm so happy! Maybe life's not as unfair as I thought."

"Yes, Drover, and behind every silver lining, there's a golden pot."

"Yeah, and every pot has a chicken in it."

"Right. And every chicken must cross the road."

His smile faded. "I wonder why."

"What?"

"Why does a chicken cross the road?"

I chuckled. "That's obvious, isn't it?"

"Not to me."

I began pacing. "Well, a chicken crosses the road . . . When a chicken takes it upon himself to cross a road or trail . . . Drover, I'm afraid we're out of time."

"Oh drat."

"And please try to control your naughty language. Don't forget your new position."

"Oh smurkle."

"That's better." I paused and glanced up at the dark clouds. "What was the point of this conversation?"

"Alfred called me a naughty dog and it broke my heart."

"Right, and we cleared that up. You're happy now and you're going to stop drawing me into these ridiculous conversations. I'm a very busy dog and I don't have time to speculate on why chickens cross roads."

"Well, you don't need to get mad."

"I'm not mad. But Drover, I came down here with something important in mind. Now I don't remember what it was. Furthermore, it has suddenly occurred to me that this entire conversation has been . . . loony. Meaningless. This has happened before, Drover, and it troubles me that we continue to carry on loony conversations. Does that bother you?"

He grinned. "No, I kind of enjoy it."

"You enjoy being a loon?"

"Oh, you're never alone when you're with somebody else. It's almost like having company."

"What?"

"I said . . . let me think here. I said, being alone's almost like owning a company, but you have to pay interest on a loan."

Seconds passed as I stared into his eyes. "Oh. Yes, of course." I paced away and tried to shake the vapors out of my head. I still couldn't remember . . .

At that very moment, Drover leaped to his feet and pointed off to the northwest. "Oh look, there's a pretty rainbow. Let's go look for the pot of chicken."

That was it! The rainbow. I had gotten so involved in Drover's personal tragedy that I had forgotten all about Pete's slip of the tongue. "Wait a minute, that was my idea. During my interrogation of the cat, he . . . Wait a minute. What was that you just said about the pot of chicken?"

"Well, let's see here." He rolled his eyes and chewed his lip. "At the end of every rainbow, there's a pot. A pot of chicken."

"Hmmm. I'd always heard that it was a pot of . . . something. Gold."

"No, I think it's chicken. Who'd want to eat gold?"

"Good point. I hadn't thought of that. Maybe it's a golden pot that contains a boiled chicken. That would explain the business about the gold, wouldn't it? Yes, of course. The pieces of the puzzle are falling into place." I glanced over both shoulders and lowered my voice. "Soldier, let's go get that treasure, but don't forget, it was my idea."

With that, we launched ourselves into the evening breeze and went streaking out to claim our rightful share of the Potted Chicken. All at once, Drover's loony conversation became a distant memory, and once again I found myself unmurshed in meaningful work—solving the Case of the Fabled Potted Chicken. *Immersed,* let us say.

With the damp wind blowing in my face, I felt whole again—sane, restored, invigorated. Suddenly I remembered why I had gone into Security Work, and why I would never allow myself to be drawn into another conversation with my lunatic assistant.

Anyway, I was in my element now, back on the job, charging out into the growing darkness to do brave and noble things—and to seize the Fabled Treasure of the Potted Chicken. You've heard of it, I'm sure, the Fabled Treasure of the Potted Chicken. Legends of the ancient Malarkeys and Babushkas had told of a fabulous treasure, don't you see, which could be found at the west end of a rainbow.

Why the west end? Nobody knew the answer to that, but for centuries dogs in America and England and Harmonica and other distant lands had searched in vain for the elusive treasure—a fat boiled chicken in a pot of purest gold. Over the years, thousands of dogs had lost their lives searching for the treasure, and now, by sheer chance and luck, it had come within the grisp of our grasp.

On and on we charged. We could see it up ahead, a big beautiful rainbow, and the west end of it had come to rest right in the middle of our horse pasture!

"There it is, Drover, straight ahead! Now all we have to do is claim it and eat the chicken."

"What about the pot?"

"If we're still hungry after the chicken, maybe we'll eat the pot."

"I'm getting tired, and my leg's killing me."

"Courage, Drover. Just a little farther. You can do it. Gut it out and make it hurt."

"It does."

"Great. Pain is our fuel, son, it's the secret elixative that drives us in this crazy business. We live on pain, we thrive on pain, we . . ."

Huh?

We had reached the middle of the horse pasture, the very spot where the treasure was supposed to be. And there we found . . . sagebrush?

I cut my eyes from side to side. "Drover, something very strange is going on here."

"Yeah," he whispered, "there's two coyotes standing right over there, and they look hungry."

HUH?

You'll never guess . . . I'm sorry, but we'll have to skip this next part.

Too scary.

CHAPTER SIX

# Caution:
# Cannibal Zone!

We don't want to get anyone hurt or scared out of their wits. Or crushed by disappointment.

See, by the time we reached the middle of the horse pasture . . . do I dare reveal this? Maybe it'll be all right, but I warn you, it's going to come as a shock.

Okay, by the time we so-forthed, the treasure *was gone.* No kidding, it had evaporized into thin hair. Thin *air,* I should say. It had evaporized into thin air, leaving us with nothing but sagebrush, beargrass, and spirits that had been crushed by the two-by-fours and rafters of our fallen dreams.

Our treasure had vanished. Perhaps it had been stolen right from under our noses. Had Pete done it? Yes, of course, I should have known! And now, as we stood in the growing twilight, we felt the crushing weight of broken dreams.

And suddenly we understood how *they* must have felt, those ancient Babushkas and Balonians and Muffwuffians who had sought the elusive treasure and, like us, had seen their dreams collapse like a rickety chicken house around their ears.

It was a dark moment for the elite forces of the Security Division, but not so dark that we couldn't see two hungry yellow-eyed cannibals staring at us. We saw them very well. Had they beat us to the treasure? No. As Drover had pointed out, they looked hungry.

I swallowed down the bitter taste of defeat and turned to my assistant. "Drover, I don't want to alarm you, but we have cannibals at oh-three-zero-zero. I suggest we go straight into Cannibal Countermeasures."

His teeth were clacking. "W-what does that m-m-mean?"

"It means," I shot a glance over my shoulder and saw that they were approaching, "it means that we're going to deny everything."

"You m-mean, about the t-t-t-treasure?"

"Yes, exactly. We'll deny any knowledge of the treasure. If that doesn't work, we'll deny knowledge of everything else—us, them, the world, the entire universe. Our story will be that we really don't exist and this is only a movie. The movie's over and it's time for them to go home. What do you think?"

"I d-don't think it'll w-w-work."

"Stop clacking your teeth. You know that annoys me."

"I c-c-can't h-help it. I'm s-s-scared of c-c-coyotes."

"So what? Everyone's s-s-scared of c-c-coyotes. The imp-p-portant th-thing is t-to ... Is that you c-c-clacking again or is it m-m-me?"

"I th-think it w-w-was y-you."

"Hmmm, y-y-yes. As I w-was s-s-saying, c-clacking is a perfectly n-n-n-natural reaction and it's e-e-even g-g-good for the d-d-d-digestion."

"How could it be good for the digestion? Hey! I'm not clacking anymore. I conquered my fear! Are you proud of me?"

I gave the runt a withering glare. "D-d-drover, s-s-sometimes I th-think you're trying to make a m-m-m-m-mockery of m-m-my ... shhhh! H-h-here they come. I'll d-d-do the t-t-talking."

"Well, you'd better quit clacking, or they'll know you're scared."

"W-will you sh-sh-shut your l-l-little t-t-trap?"

I rushed to the computer of my mind and typed

in the commands to Erase All Clacking Files. I had to hurry. As Drover had noted, it wouldn't be good for me to address the cannibals with a speech implement in my voice. Impediment. Wh-wh-whatever. I gazed at Data Control's vast screen and waited. Seconds passed, then a message appeared:

*"French fries or hash browns?"*

I shot a glance at the coyotes—Rip and Snort, as you might have guessed. They were only five feet away. In desperation, I retyped the message: "Erase the clacking files, you idiot, or we'll all be eaten by cannibals!!! If we go down, you'll go down with us."

A message flashed across the screen: *"Peanut butter sandwiches are slightly higher west of Observatory Park."*

In a flash of anger, I screamed, "You moron! At a time like this, do I care about peanut butter sandwiches?"

I noticed that Drover was staring at me. "Are you talking to me?"

I whirled around. "No. Yes. I'm not sure. Did you just say something about peanut butter sandwiches?"

"Well, let me think. I don't remember. What did I say?"

"You said . . . I can't remember. No, wait. You

said they're slightly higher west of . . . Mount Rushmore, I think it was."

"Nope, that wasn't me. I would have said they're made out of peanut butter."

The coyote brothers were almost on top of us now, but I couldn't deal with them until I got to the bottom of Drover's barrel. I sensed that there was a clue here that might send the case careening in a new direction. "Why would you say that?"

"'Cause they are. Everyone knows that peanut butter sandwiches are made of peanut butter."

"Right, and if everyone knows it, why would you bother to say it? And why would you ignore the part about Mount Rushmore? Don't you care about our great presidents?"

"You're not clacking anymore."

"That's no excuse, and don't argue with me. The point is . . ." Hmmm. I wasn't clacking anymore. It appeared that Data Control had come through in the crutch. I typed in one last message, just before all our communications were cut off: *"Hash browns, you dork."*

Then I turned to face the . . . yipes, the toothy grins of the cannibal brothers. I took a moment to collect my thoughts and seize a breath of fresh air, then beamed them a broad, friendly smile that spoke of the Brotherhood of All Dogs and Doglike Creatures.

"Hi, guys. Nice evening, huh? You bet. How's the family? Great. Let me go straight to the point and say that we know nothing about the Fabled Treasure of the Potted Chicken. Honest. And since we know nothing about it, it's obvious that we're not out here looking for it."

They gave me blank yellow stares. I plunged on. "Furthermore, we deny any knowledge of anything. We didn't do it, you can't prove a thing, you have no case, and, well, I guess we'd better be moving along." To Drover, I whispered, "Start edging back toward headquarters."

He was gazing up at the clouds. "What?"

I had to raise my voice. "I said, back toward the starting edge of headquarters, and hurry, before these guys get suspicious. Move. Oh, and try to act normal."

"I've been trying all my life."

"Good point. Forget normal. Try to act unconcerned, calm, confident. Whistle."

"You know, I never could whistle. My sister whistled all the time and I was always jealous."

"All right, don't whistle, and I don't care about your sister."

"She was the sweetest girl I ever met. How could you not care about her?"

"Do you want to talk about your sister or live to see another day? Start edging toward headquarters, and hum."

"Hum?"

"Yes, Drover, hum. Hummmmm."

"Oh, I get it now." He gave me a wink. "Hum hum hum. Hum hummy humbug. Humly hummering hummington. Humblebee hummeration humming ho-hum."

This seemed to be working. The brothers hadn't moved, and were staring at us as though . . . well, as though they couldn't believe their eyes and ears. That was fine. They were falling right into my trap.

I turned and gave them a wave of farewell. "Well, guys, see you around. Tell the family hello."

Suddenly, and I mean in a flash, they were standing in front of us, bristled up and blocking our path. Snort spoke. "What means all this hum-hummery-humblebug stuff?"

"It means . . . well, it means that Drover is a happy little dog."

"Ha. Rip and Snort not give a hoot for happy little dog."

"I see. Well, at a deeper level, Snort, the humming symbolizes our, uh, feelings of confidence, don't you see. We feel good about who we are, and along those very same lines, we feel good about who *you* are. Isn't it good that we all feel good about, uh, who we are?"

Snort stared at me for a moment, then clubbed me over the head with his paw. "Hunk talk stupider and stupidest. Rip and Snort not give a hoot for feeling good. What means talk about Treasurous Potty Chicken?"

I picked myself off the ground and straightened my ears. "I . . . I don't know what you're talking about." He raised his paw to club me again. "Oh, that! Okay, here we go. You mean the Fabled Treasure of the Potted Chicken?"

He nodded. "Tabled Treasurous of Potty Chicken. Rip and Snort got big hungry for potty chicken."

"It's *Potted Chicken*. Pot-ted. Chicken in a pot." Snort raised his paw again. "Okay, okay, have it your way. It's Potty Chicken."

The brothers exchanged winks and chuckles, and Snort said, "Ha! Hunk not fool Rip and Snort with dummy talk and change up words."

"I guess not. So you're demanding that I tell you about the Potted . . . eh, the Potty Chicken? Is that what I'm hearing you say?" They nodded. "What if I told you it was secret information?" They stared. "Don't you even care?" They stared. "Look, Snort, if I gave you the secret, you'd probably go right out and steal our chicken."

"Rip and Snort berry good for steal chicken."

"Yes, but that would be cheating."

"Ha! Rip and Snort berry good for cheat too, better cheatists in whole world."

"Yes, but then everyone would call you a chicken cheater. Is that how you want to live your life?"

"Coyote brothers wanting to live life with tummy full of chicken—or dog."

My mouth was suddenly dry. "I see your point. Okay, guys, you leave me no choice. I guess I'll have to tell you everything."

And with that, I let it all spill out, all the classified information I had dragged out of the cat, and had spent so many long hours and months piecing together. When I had finished, they knew everything, every detail—that at the west end of every rainbow, there sits a golden pot of boiled chicken.

Our secret was lost. And so were our hopes of ever finding the Fabled Treasure of the Potted Chicken. On the other hand . . .

Heh heh. I had every confidence that the cannibals would go streaking off to find the elusive west end of the rainbow, thus leaving us free to make our escape.

Heh heh.

Pretty clever, huh?

# CHAPTER SEVEN

# I Issue
# a Challenge

Even though I had found a way of turning this security disaster into a silver lining, it was with a heavy heart that I had spilled the milk.

I mean, every dog dreams of the day when he can eat a whole chicken all by himself, and we're talking about *free* chicken, one that doesn't have to be chased all over the ranch and mugged and defeathered and so forth. And don't forget that attacking chickens was a serious crime on our outfit, and it could get a guy in big trouble with Sally May.

She fed those chickens and got twelve eggs a day from them, don't you know, and she took a dim view of any dog who made a habit of . . . well, eating them, shall we say. Why, the last time I'd gone after one of her chickens . . .

Wait, hold it, stop, whoa! Strike that last sentence from the record. It's not only inflammatory, but it creates a false impression of the truth. In other words, I was misquoted.

For the record, let me restate my Position on Chickens. Chickens are dumb birds who . . . slurp, slurp . . . were placed on this earth to be . . . slurp, slurp . . . funny, my mouth starts watering every time I think about . . . slurp, slop . . . but back to the point, chickens were put on this earth to be . . . slurp, slop, slorp . . .

I can't go on with this. Sorry. The strain is just too much. Maybe you can finish up my Position on . . . slurp, slurp . . . never mind.

Okay, where was I? Free chicken, there we go. Free chicken is every dog's dream and fondish wist. But the coyote brothers had changed all that.

When I had emptied my soul and divulged all the classified information that would allow the brothers to steal our Fabled Free Potted Chicken at the End of the Rainbow, I felt a terrible sense of guilt and emptiness.

I turned to Drover. "I'm sorry, son, but it was us or the chicken."

He was staring at the clouds. "What?"

"I said, I'm sorry. I had to do it."

His eyes drifted down and he gave me his

usual silly grin. "Oh, hi. What did you do?"

"I spilled the beans. I told them everything. They beat it out of me."

"Boy, I love beans."

My lips quivered as I tried to think of something to say to this . . . this nitwit, this moron of indescribable proportions. I could think of nothing to say. The boat of my mind had been swamped by the roaring sea of his . . . never mind.

I whirled away from him and saw . . . huh? The coyote brothers were . . . laughing? I was stunned. The boat of my mind, which had so recently been swamped by the waves of Drover's blathering nincompoopery, was now dashed upon the rocks of . . . something.

"Hey Snort, I just gave you some incredibly valuable information, and now you're laughing. What's the deal?"

"Deal is that Rip and Snort not believe one word of big phooey lies about potty chicken and rainbows, ho ho."

"You mean . . . you mean you don't believe in chickens?"

He stopped laughing and gave me a menacing glare. "Coyote believe in chicken but not believe in rainbow."

I searched their faces. "How could you not

believe in rainbows? There's one right over there, plain as day."

They exchanged smirks. "Ha! Hunk-dog got big stupid in head. Rainbow not real, just color in air. Rip and Snort chase rainbow many times and never catch one."

"Hmm, yes, of course. We had the same, uh, problem. It moved."

They took a step toward me. "Potty Chicken just big phooey lie, another trick Hunk try to pull on Rip and Snort."

I began backing up. "Wait a minute, fellas, this is all news to me, and also a terrible shock. I mean, I thought I was giving you . . . no kidding, we got that information from a very reliable source and I want to assure you . . . Drover, do something! Hey Snort, I think I can explain everything, honest. See, we've got this cat on the place . . ."

They were licking their chops by this time and things were not looking good. "Rip and Snort not get potty chicken for supper, but maybe find something gooder and goodest, oh boy!"

"Listen, guys, speaking of cats, how about we work a deal on a nice fat kitty, huh? How does that sound?"

They shook their heads in unison. "Not got cat. Got two dummy ranch dogs, ho ho."

"That's not funny, Snort, and I must warn you that Drover has a terrible temper." That didn't work. Drover had already collapsed in fright. The cannibals just laughed. "Okay, singing. You guys love to sing, right? Everybody knows that, so why don't we, well, burst into song?"

They shook their heads in unison. "Guys too hungry for burp into song."

"Yeah, but I said *burst,* not burp. There's a huge difference."

"Coyote berry expert at burping and not give a hoot for huge different."

"Okay, then . . ." I took a gulp of air and plunged into my very last idea. It was a little crazy, but it was my last shot. "Okay, Snort, just for that, I challenge you fleabags to a contest of courage, skill, and brute strength."

They stopped. Their ears shot up. They exchanged puzzled looks. "What means, brute strinks?"

"*Strength,* Snort. Strength, as in strong. It means the strength of a brute. Only a heartless brute could win this contest, and you guys probably aren't tough enough to enter, much less win."

Snort pounded himself on the chest and roared. "Coyote got plenty brute! Coyote bruter and brutest, and got bunch of strinks, too. Coyote beat up whole world with bruter strinks."

"Well, we'll just see about that. Drover, wake up. We'll need you to judge this." The runt let out a moan. I marched over and kicked him on the bohunkus. "Hey, wake up and smell the cobras."

He lifted his head and cracked one eye. "Help, murder, Mayday, I'm scared of snakes, oh my leg!"

"Forget the leg. Wake up and pay attention. I've got something cooking here."

His eyes popped open. "The chicken?"

"No, not the chicken. While you were fainting, we learned that the chicken business was just another of Pete's famous lies. I should have known."

"Oh drat."

"Drover, please try to control your naughty language."

"Oh piffle."

"That's better. What we have cooking here is . . ." I gave him a cunning wink of the eye, ". . . a P-L-A-N."

He twisted his head and stared at me. "Something's wrong with your eye."

"Drover, something's fixing to be wrong with your . . . Think, Drover, concentrate. I have a P-L-A-N."

His eyes went blank. "That's not how you spell chicken. You spell chicken with a C-H."

"I know that, you . . ." I fought to control my temper. "P-L-A-N."

"Plane? You've got an airplane, and we're going to climb in and fly away so the coyotes won't eat us? Oh, I'm so happy!"

The air hissed out of my lungs. I shot a glance over at the brothers. They were jumping up and down, showing each other their biceps, and getting warmed up for the big contest. I turned back to Drover.

"Forget the spelling, Drover. I have a *plan*."

"Oh, I thought you had a plane and I was so excited about taking a ride. I've never ridden in an airplane. Now I'm all disappointed."

Once again, my lips were twitching in . . . something. Rage. Anger. Unspeakable frustration in the face of chaos. "Drover, sometimes I think I hate you."

"No, 'cause if you'd ate me, I wouldn't be here."

"Will you shut your trap! Now sit up and pay attention, and stand by to," I dropped my voice to a whisper, "make a run for it."

"What? I couldn't hear that."

"Make a run for it."

"Right now?"

I saw a small hackberry tree nearby, walked over to it, and banged my head against it three times. I returned to the dunce and said, "Just pay attention and be ready to move out."

"Oh, okay. I can handle that."

The brothers were warmed up for the big contest. They were getting restless, so I turned my attention back to them. "Okay, fellas, we're ready to begin this deadly contest, from which only one of us will return alive."

Snort's eyes widened with glee. "Uh! Sound gooder and goodest. Rip and Snort not scared even little teenie bit."

"Well, you ought to be scared. This contest will make anything you've ever done look like a chick purchnick."

"Uh! Coyote eat chick but not believe in potty chicken."

"Actually, I meant to say 'church picnic.'"

He bashed me over the head with his paw. "Hunk talk too much. Rip and Snort not give a hoot for chicky churchnik. Hurry up and start big contest."

I picked myself up off the ground. "Okay, guys, this is it. We're fixing to engage in a contest called the Ha-Ha Game." They gave me scowls. "The Deadly Dangerous Ha-Ha Game." They nodded and grinned. "Here are the rules. I'll start off with a 'ha,' then we go back and forth, and each one of us will add another 'ha' to what the other one said. The point is to keep from laughing. You got it?"

Snort shook his head. "Sound stupid, not deadlier or dangerous."

"Well, it starts off easy, but after it goes on for hours and hours, it becomes a real test of strength and endurance. And don't forget, only one of us will come back alive. Ready?"

The brothers lowered their heads and took a wide stance. They were ready. So was I.

Would you care to see a transcript of the contest? We seldom do that, you know, because . . . well, we just don't, mainly because of the kids. The children. We wouldn't want to expose them to toxic levels of violence and bloodshed and noise and all the other stuff that comes out of these deadly dangerous contests.

What do you think?

I guess we could give it a try. If our readings on the Toxometer get too far into the red zone, we'll just shut 'er down and go on to something else.

Ready? Here we go. Here's the actual true transcript of the Deadly and Dangerous Ha-Ha Game.

# The Deadly
# Ha-Ha Game

## Actual True Transcript

### Deadly and Dangerous Ha-Ha Game #1
### Wednesday Evening 8:37:24

*PLEASE NOTE! What you are about to read is an actual, factual, word-for-word transcription of an epic battle conducted on the ranch, on the very evening it occurred. The names used are the actual names of the combatants, and no effort has been made to hide their identities. They include, in the order of their appearance, Hank the Cowdog, Head of Ranch Security, a local hero adored by lady dogs all over Texas; and Rip and Snort, two fleabag cannibal brothers.*

*The transcript is uncut and uncensored. Viewers, listeners, and observers should be warned that it might contain scenes that are terrifying and language that some viewers might find monotonous. In the event of a post-battle reaction, please consult a doctor, veterinarian, or licensed plumber.*

HANK: Ha.

R&S: Ha, ha.

HANK: Ha, ha, ha.

R&S: Ha, ha, ha, ha.

HANK: Ha, ha, ha, ha, ha.

R&S: Ha, ha, ha, ha, ha, ha.

HANK: Ha, ha, ha, ha, ha, ha, ha.

R&S: Ha, ha, ha, ha, ha, ha, ha, ha, ha, ha, ha, ha, ha, ha, ha, ho-ho, hee-hee, har-har, ha, ha, ha, ha, ha, ha, ho-ho-ho, hee-hee-hee, har-har-har . . . etc.

*PLEASE NOTE! Transcript ends at this point, when the cannibal brothers collapsed in spasms of insane laughter and were unable to continue the battle, leaving Hank the Cowdog the undisputed champion.*

### End of Ha-Ha Game Transcript

Do you get it now? Pretty smart, huh? You bet it was. I had lured the dumbbell coyote brothers right into a clever trap, and they fell for it like a ton of hooks, lines, and sinkers. See, once they got into that ha-ha business, they started laughing, and once they started laughing, they couldn't stop.

The mind of a dog is a frightening thing.

Heh heh.

And once I saw that the fleabags had been immobilized by their own laughter, I gave them a smile and a wave, and walked away from the pile made of their squirming bodies. Drover was waiting for me, and his eyes were wide with amazement.

"How'd you do that?"

"It was easy, but never mind. We don't have

time to discuss it. While they're out of commission, we need to hurry back to headquarters."

We left the brothers screaming with laughter and rolling around on the ground, and went streaking back to headquarters. Even though I had whipped the stuffings out of the cannibal brothers and had become undisputed Ha-Ha Champion of the World, I didn't want to become careless or cocky.

I mean, just because you're the smartest, toughest, best-looking dog in the whole Texas Panhandle doesn't mean that you can get coyless about carrots. Careless about coyotes, I should say. They're stupid brutes, but they do have a kind of crude intelligence that makes them dangerous adversaries. Remember the wise old saying . . .

Never pick up a snake until the fat lady sings.

Never pick up a snake until the fat lady cuts off its head.

Never pick up a fat lady while she's singing.

There's some wise old saying about snakes and fat ladies, but I don't care about it and I'm not going to mention it.

Wait. I think I've got it. Never pick up a fat snake . . .

Maybe I can paraphrase the wise old saying. The point is that you can ruin your back picking up fat ladies, and some of them will slap the snot out of you, and dead snakes aren't always as dead as they . . .

Just skip it. I'm sorry I brought it up.

Where were we? Wherever we were, it had nothing to do with fat ladies or dead snakes. Oh yes, our escape.

I had just made the decision not to be careless or cocky about my huge triumph over the dumbbell coyotes. Hencely, instead of strolling back to headquarters, we punched in the Rocket Dog Program, went roaring through the horse pasture, and came to a gentle landing on the gravel drive in front of the machine shed.

Only then did I dare to do what any normal American dog would have done. I looked back toward the horse pasture, stuck out my tongue, made monkey ears, and yelled scorn and abuse at the coyotes.

"There, you losers, and the next time you dare to mess with Hank the Cowdog, you'll get the same treatment—or something worse! Nyee, nyee, nyee! You couldn't catch a flea on a grandpa's knee! What a couple of morons! I can't believe you were dumb enough to fall for that trick."

I was just getting warmed up, I mean, this was fun! If you can't be an unbearable winner, what's the point of winning? But I noticed that Drover was getting moon-eyed and worried.

"Hank, maybe you'd better not rub it in. I think they've quit laughing."

Sure enough, the laughter had stopped. "Oh rubbish, you worry too much. They're out there in the pasture and we're here at ranch headquarters, and everybody knows that coyotes won't come into ranch headquarters. They're scared of people."

He glanced down at the house. It was dark. "Yeah, but the people have already gone to bed."

"The odds are on our side, Drover, and the problem with you is that you've had very little experience at winning. You don't know how to act."

"I guess you're right. What are you supposed to do?"

I patted the little mutt on the shoulder. "Listen to this. I'll give you your first lesson on how to be a winner." And with that, I did a little number called "Be a Winner."

**Be a Winner**

Let's start with a basic lesson or two.
Life's a contest, son, and everything we do
Is a struggle, a battle, a game to the end,
And the ob-ject-ive is always to win.
Be a winner.
Be a winner.

Now, playing the game is the easiest part,
Just figure out the rules and start at the
    start.
Play by the rules, if it suits your design,
Or cheat, if you must, that'll be just fine, but
Be a winner.
Be a winner.

Now, once you've notched up a victory
The fun begins, as you will see.
The crowd'll cheer, you'll beam a smile
Of humbleness—for a little while.
Be a winner.
Be a winner.

Good sportsmanship gets old real quick,
And humble pie can make you sick.
The time has come to create a buzz.
You're the coolest dog who ever was.
Be a winner.
Be a winner.

Start things off by crossing your eyes,
Stick out your tongue and yell, "Hey, guys,
Here's some monkey ears, get out of my road!
I won, you lost, and your momma's a toad!"
Be a winner.
Be a winner.

There's a moral here, some great advice:
There's no point in winning if you have
    to be nice.
So do what you can to drive 'em berserk.
Be obnoxious and rude, rub it in, be a jerk.
Be a winner, heh heh, yeah,
Be a winner.

When I was done, Drover grinned. "Gosh, thanks. That helps a bunch."

"Good. Great. I'm always glad to help you through life's little trials."

"Yeah, but I still don't understand what you said to the coyotes that made 'em laugh so hard. Now that we're safe, maybe you could tell me."

I glanced over both shoulders, just to be sure we weren't being watched, and lowered my voice. "I'll tell you, but you've got to promise to keep it a secret. We don't want Pete getting hold of this information."

He promised to keep it a secret, and I told him about the Ha-Ha Game. Naturally, he was impressed. "I'll be derned. How'd you ever think of that?"

"It's an old spy trick, Drover. I've been saving it back for an emergency."

"Boy, it sure worked. Do you reckon we could try it out, just you and me?"

I swept my gaze around the headquarters compound. Everything was quiet. "Sure, I guess we've got time to run through it once. You want to kick it off or shall I?"

"Oh, you'd better do it. I might mess up."

"Good thinking. Don't forget, the point is to keep yourself from laughing. Okay, here we go. Ha."

"Ha ha."

"Ha ha ha."

"Ha ha ha ha."

"Ha ha ha ha ha."

"Uh-oh," he giggled, "I'm fixing to lose it. Ha ha ha ha ha ha ha ha, hee hee, ho ho!"

When he lost it, so did I. I mean, when a guy is standing there in front of you, laughing himself silly, it's hard to maintain Iron Discipline. "Ha ha ha ha, hee hee hee, ho ho ho, ha ha ha!"

Yes sir, we lost it, both of us, and we're talking about falling down and rolling around in the dirt, is how much we lost it. I hadn't laughed so hard in years. It was kind of a touching moment, actually, the elite forces of the Security Division taking time out of our busy schedules to share . . .

HUH?

Rip and Snort?

# Oops

What were they . . . Hey, it was common knowledge that coyotes never . . .

They not only looked hungry, but also mad, very mad. Oops. Maybe we shouldn't have given them monkey ears.

"Hey ha ha, Drover ha ha, do you ha ha see what I ha ha see?"

"Ha ha yeah. I thought they were ha ha out in the ha ha horse pasture."

"Ha ha right, but they're ha ha here now ha ha. And you ha ha know what ha ha? I can't stop ha ha ha laughing."

"Ha ha, me neither ha ha."

"Ha ha Drover, I think we need to . . . ha ha ha ha ha ha."

"Get ha ha out of here?"

"Ha ha right. Because if we ha ha don't, they're going to . . . ha ha ha ha."

"Ha ha eat us?"

"Right. Yes. Ha ha ha ha ha."

"Ha ha! Hank, that's not ha ha funny."

"I know, so stop . . . ha ha ha ha . . . laughing."

The brothers had been watching us with big smirks on their toothy mouths, but then Snort licked his chops and rumbled, "Ha ha, now dummy ranch dogs die laughing and make supper for Rip and Snort, ha ha!"

That did it. I mean, you talk about something that will kill a party. Those words hit us like a bucket of cold water in the face, and suddenly we weren't laughing any moron. Any more, let us say. "Quick, Drover, into the machine shed!"

One step ahead of the cannibals, we dove through the crack between the sliding doors of the machine shed. Whew! Boy, that had been a close one. I knew the coyotes would never . . . I mean, they had never dared set foot in the machine shed because . . . well, think about it. The machine shed was full of human smells and it just wasn't the kind of place . . .

Yipes! *They followed us inside!*

"Run, Drover, head for the deepest, darkest corner and hide!"

"Help, murder, Mayday, oh my leg!"

While Drover squeaked and moaned, I fired off several blasts of Over the Shoulder Barking, and we both cut a hole through the darkness and headed for the northeast corner. Getting there turned out to be no can of cookies.

Piece of cookie.

Can of worms.

Piece of cake, shall we say, because the machine shed was full of junk—not just the tools and bolt bins and welding equipment you'd expect to find in a machine shed, but also stuff you'd never expect to find. A table lamp. A stack of dishes. Alfred's old high chair. Loper's canvas-covered canoe. And five hundred and thirty-seven old paint cans that had been there since Sally May had painted the house.

Fellers, I sure felt bad about blasting a hole through all those treasures, but with two cannibals hot on my trail, I did it anyway, and we're talking about a lot of crashing and banging. At last, we reached the northwest corner, as far from the door as we could get, and took cover under . . . something. What was that thing? An old coffee table, I suppose, with just enough room for me and Drover to squeeze ourselves underneath.

Then and only then did I dare catch a breath

and whisper, "I think we're safe. It's so dark back here, those guys'll never..."

It was then that my ears picked up the sound of ... sniffing. A lot of sniffing, and it seemed to be ... uh ... coming in our direction.

"Drover, do you hear something?"

"Yeah. Sniffing, and it's not me."

"Right, and it's not me either. I have a hunch that it's the coyotes."

"I was afraid of that. I guess we shouldn't have played the Ha-Ha Game."

"I agree. It's a powerful technique and it was foolish of us to mess around with it. Now we've stapped into our own truck."

"What?"

"I said, we've stepped into our own trap. For you see, Drivel..."

"My name's Drover."

"I know your name, Driver, but I'm so nervous I can hardly talk. For you see, we can't depend on darkness to hide us. Those coyotes aren't using their eyes. They're following their keen sense of smell, and it's only a matter of time..."

The silence was ripped by the sound of Snort's voice. "Uh! Lost trail of dummy dogs. Now everything smell like ... paint."

Did you hear that? What a struck of loke! The

brothers had followed our scent right up to the five hundred and thirty-seven half-empty cans of paint and . . . and I had thought of that all along, no kidding, losing our scent around the paint cans, I mean, it had been an obvious ploy, and it had worked like a . . .

But all at once, I began picking up a new sound. Clacking. I lifted my ears and swiveled them around. The sound was close. It was coming from . . .

"Drover, for crying out loud, will you stop clacking your teeth!"

"I c-c-can't h-help it! I'm so s-s-s-scared . . ."

The jagged hacksaw laughter of the coyote brothers cut through the gloomy darkness of the dark gloom. It sent cold chills down my backbone. Then . . .

"Aha! Rip and Snort not need smell dummy dogs no more. Got sound coming from back of shed. Sound berry much like clacking tooths."

To which Rip gave his only statement of the night. "Uh!"

Once again, we've come to a part in the story that might be too scary for the average reader. I mean, we were trapped in the machine shed, right? If Rip and Snort caught us back there, we were dead meat, history, supper for cannibals. Everyone down at the house was asleep, so we were totally on our own.

I'd say things were looking pretty bad. If we got caught and eaten, there would be no more story. And you know what? That's just what happened. We got caught and eaten by cannibals, and that's it.

I know you paid a lot of money for this book, but what can I say?

Sorry. Shall we discuss funerals? Maybe not, because when coyotes finish a meal, there isn't much left for a funeral, so I guess . . .

No, wait, hold everything!

You won't believe this. I didn't believe it. It was unbelievable, and yet . . .

Okay, here's the deal. When Snort heard Drover's teeth clacking, his powerful ears tracked the sound to our hiding place. He knew we were trapped. It made him so happy, he was bubbling over with wild cannibal joy and he cut loose with a big laugh. "HA!"

And Rip, who was just as joyful, said, "Ha ha!"

"Ha ha ha!"

"Ha ha ha ha!"

"Ha ha . . . not start stupid Ha-Ha Game again . . . ha ha ha!"

"Ha ha ha ha ha ha!"

"Got to quit ha ha, not have time for . . . ha ha ha ha ha ha ha!"

Can you believe it? The dummies got sucked

into the powerful gravitational pull of the Ha- Ha Game, and *they'd done it to themselves!* Their laughing and hooting rattled the tin on the roof, and paint cans went clattering in all directions as they rolled across the floor. The coyotes, that is. They were rolling around on the floor, but so were the paint cans.

When I realized what I was hearing, I turned to my assistant. "Drover, we've just pulled our coconuts out of the fire. Against incredible odds, we've been saved."

"Oh good! I sure like coconuts."

"I didn't say coconuts. I said chestnuts."

"I never ate one."

"Nor have I, but apparently you roast them over an open fire, and there's an old expression . . ."

"You reckon we ought to get out of here?"

I aimed a withering glare at the piece of darkness where I thought Drover should be. "Who's in charge around here? And who's going to correct your mistakes if I don't do it?"

"Well . . ."

"I'm sorry, we're out of time. We need to get out of here."

"I never thought of that."

"Okay, listen up, here's the plan. Between here and the door, we'll use the Bulldozer Program. Just lower your head and batter your way through anything in your way, especially if it's hairy and big."

"I hear that."

"When we reach the door, we'll set a speed course of one-five-zero-zero, go to Full Flames on all engines, and head straight for the house."

"What about the fence?"

"It doesn't matter. Jump it, go under it, take it out, whatever. The fence is irrelevent."

"Irrelevant."

"What?"

"I said, the fence is irrelevant."

"That's what I just said. The fence is irrelevent and quit butting into my strategic planning. We'll take out the fence and then go straight into Alert and Alarm. I think our friends at the house will want to know that their dogs have been attacked by savage coyotes."

"Yeah, or they'll be mad 'cause we woke 'em up."

"Ha! I don't . . ."

"Ha ha!"

"Ha ha ha! Don't start that or we'll never get out of here!"

"Ha ha ha ha! I can't stop, Hank, help, it's got me again!"

"Ha ha ha ha ha! You stay here and laugh all you want, pal. I'm leaving!"

You probably find it hard to believe that I was able to overcome the fierce gravitational pull of the Ha-Ha Game, which was sucking me into its swirling center. Well, it was tough, I can tell you that, and most of your ordinary dogs wouldn't have had the iron discipline to tear themselves out of the grisp of its deadly grasp. Even I had trouble. I mean, the power of that thing was just awesome.

But I got 'er done, shifted up into the Bulldozer Program, and plowed a path through objects that would have stopped a charging rhino. Boy, you should have seen it! Furniture, canoes, huge drill presses, welders, paint cans, cars, you name it, flying in all directions. When Sally May saw the damage, she would . . . but that was another problem.

I fought and clawed and battered my way to the door, and there I paused just long enough to yell, "See you around, you miserable moth-eaten . . ."

Their laughter stopped, and I could hear them coming! When will I ever learn to . . . oh well, it was spilled milk under the bridge. I dove through the door and with a blast of powerful rocket engines, went streaking down to the house.

As the fence loomed up before me, I got a warning light from Data Control: *"Fence. Cancel, ignore, or try again?"*

With only seconds left, I typed in my reply:

*"Watch this, and mind your own business."*

I took a deep seat, braced myself, and . . . BONK!

Okay, that fence proved to be a little stouter than we had supposed and we decided to leave it, uh, standing. I mean, there was no reason for . . . never mind. I made it into the yard, that's the important thing, and once there, I made a terrible discovery.

Drover wasn't behind me!

# CHAPTER TEN

# Followed
# into the Yard!

**D**rover wasn't behind me because he was already in the yard. Somehow, through some flupe of luck, he had . . . but never mind the flupe of luck. Fluke of luck, that is. The good news was that he was safe. The bad news was that Rip and Snort were swaggering down the hill toward the yard.

"Drover, how many times have I told you not to get ahead of your leader?"

"I don't know. Five?"

"No, not five. At least a hundred times I've told you that every mission has a leader, and the leader should always go first. I am Head of Ranch Security. I am our leader! You've undermired the whole purpose of our mission."

"Yeah, but I was scared."

"Being scared is not an excuse. If we don't have discipline in our ranks, what do we have?"

"Two coyotes at the yard gate."

"What? Oh, them. Forget the coyotes, Drover. They'll come right up to the fence and stop. We've seen this tactic before and they've never come into the yard. The point here is that you seem determined to turn our elite unit into a leaderless rabble of rubble. Every unit consists of . . ."

"Hank, are you sure they won't come into the yard?"

"Positive. It would go against their nature. As I was saying, every unit consists of leaders and followers. It's impossible for me to lead our troops into battle if . . . Are you listening?"

"Sort of, but I'm watching the coyotes too, just in case."

"Trust me, Drover. If you don't trust your leaders, what do we have? What has the world come to?"

"Hank, I think they're going to jump the fence."

"Oh rubbish, they wouldn't dare come into the yard. Do you know why? In the first place, that fence is the boundary line between civilization and wilderness. Coyotes are, by their very nature, uncivilized brutes, so why would they want to come into the yard?"

"Oh, maybe they still want to eat us . . . or something."

"To that, I say phooey. It'll never happen. In the second place, Sally May would never allow coyotes in her yard."

"Yeah, she doesn't allow dogs in her yard either, but here we are."

"Exactly my point. We are the guardians of civilization. That's why we're here, and if Sally May understood the nature of our mission, I'm sure she would be glad—nay, delighted—to have us in her yard."

"Uh-oh, one of 'em just jumped the fence. Hank . . ."

"Don't argue with me. The point here is . . . What did you just say?"

"I don't remember."

"Something about . . . somebody just jumped the fence?"

"Oh yeah. One of the coyotes jumped over the fence. He's in the yard."

HUH?

I whirled away from Drover's nonsense and saw . . . I whirled back to Drover. "He can't do that."

"Yeah, but he just did."

"It's forbidden. Sally May would . . ." I whirled back to the coyotes. "Hey, you! Get out of the yard,

**97**

right this very minute! How dare you enter a civilized zone without permission!"

Snort chuckled and raised a big paw-fist. "Got plenty permission. Rip and Snort madder and maddest over stupid Ha-Ha Game."

"Oh that. Well, hey, if that's the problem, I think I can explain everything. No kidding."

"Brothers not give a hoot for no kidding." He jerked his head at Rip, and Rip jumped into the . . . gulp . . . yard. "What Hunk say now?"

"I say . . . Snort, I still say you can't do this." I turned to Drover. "They can't do this." Back to Snort. "Snort, let me point out that you are trespassing in a civilized zone, and, well, coyotes just never enter such places. It's forbidden. It isn't done. It violates all our, uh, treaties and traditions, and I'm sure you'll agree . . ."

They took a step toward us. Their respective mouths were covered with wild toothy grins.

I took a step backward. "Snort, I'm warning you. Unless you leave this yard immediately, and I mean at once, we'll be forced to take drastic action. We'll . . . we'll bark. We'll wake up the house. We'll call in the entire amassed forces of the Security Division. Would you believe that the Rottweiler Guard is waiting in their barracks?"

Snort widened his grin. "Uh-uh."

"Okay, would you believe that we have a secret weapon that's even deadlier than the Ha-Ha Game?"

"Uh-uh."

"Okay, in that case . . ." I turned to face Drover, only that turned out to be an impossible task. See, he was cowering behind my back, and when I turned to face him, he turned too, staying behind me. "Will you stand still?"

"Help!"

"How can I give you the plan if I can't see you?"

"Help!"

"Drover, this situation has gotten out of hand. We've lost the yard and we have no choice but to run for our lives. Prepare to initiate the Sell the Farm Program. Can you hear me?"

"Help!"

"On the count of three, we'll cut loose with a withering barrage of backing and start barking out of here. And remember, even though we're retreating, we don't want them to know it."

"Help!"

"One! Two!"

ZOOM! He was gone like a little white rocket streaking around the south side of the house. I gave the cannibals one last burst of barkfire, then followed my cowardly assistant in . . . well, blind retreat, might as well go ahead and admit it. We had lost all discipline, all pretense that we were the elite forces of the . . .

Hey, this was unbelievable! Coyotes had never come up into the yard. Okay, maybe once or twice before, but it was the kind of thing that rarely ever happened and we had no contagency plans for it. What could we do but run for our lives and hope that someone inside the house would come to our rescue?

And so it was that we began, well, lapping the house. On the second lap, I saw Pete's head poking out of the iris patch. "Hey, Pete, great to see you again! Listen, pal, could you come out here for a second? I've been thinking about all the mean things I've done to you, and hey, I think it's time for us to, you know, patch things up. What do you think?"

He stared at me as I raced past, then turned his eyes to the coyotes. I saw the blur of his tail and he was gone, the little sneak. Can you believe he'd turn his back on a couple of friends and just leave us to be . . . He would pay for this.

And for his phony information about the Potted Chicken. What a pack of lies. I'd never believed one word of it.

On the third lap around the house, I knew that

we were in serious trouble. We still had a slim lead
on the brotherhood, but they were gaining ground
on every lap. Sell the Farm hadn't worked, and we
had no choice but to initiate Desperate Measures—
go to Sirens and Lights, Flares and Whistles, the
whole nine yards of countermeasures that might
save our lives.

Yes, I knew we would awaken the house. Yes,
I knew that when awakened from peaceful sleep,
our human friends tended to be . . . how can I say
this? They tended to be angry and irrational. But

once they understood the seriousness of our situation, they would . . . probably be angry and irrational, but maybe they would turn their anger and irration against the cannibals, instead of their loyal dogs.

And so it was that on Lap #4 I went to Full Countermeasures. I barked. I howled. I moaned. I barked some more. What did Drover do? I'm not sure, for you see, somewhere between Laps #1 and #2, he had vanished without a trace, the little . . . How did he do that? I didn't know. If I had known, I would have tried it myself.

I mean, in the middle of a chase, how did the runt *just disappear*? And if those coyote brothers were such hot-shot trackers, why hadn't they followed Drover's scent instead of mine? Oh well.

I went to Full Countermeasures, and we're talking about loud barking that was full of distress and concern. As I approached Loper and Sally May's bedroom window on Lap #5, I heard a welcome sound.

Someone was opening the window! Oh, relief! Oh, salvation! I knew I was safe now. Loper would come flying out the window, grab a . . . whatever he might find to grab, a stick, a rock, a fence post, and he would start swinging, and coyotes would go flying in all directions.

I would be saved. I would leap into Loper's awaiting arms. He would hug me and I would lick his face. Just like old times. A great way to wind up the . . .

"Hank, if you don't shut up that dadgum barking, I'm going to come out there and kick your tail up between your shoulderblades! Now hush up and get out of the yard!"

Kick my tail . . . hey, I was the guy who was trying to save his house and yard from an invasion of cannibals! If he was keen on kicking some tails up between some shoulderblades, how about if he started with Rip and Snort? Or maybe he didn't care if the coyotes ate his loyal dog, and then ate all the shrubberies and flowers in the yard, and then ate the house too, huh?

You know, in some ways this is a lousy job. How's a guy supposed to be Head of Ranch Security if the people he's trying to protect don't . . . never mind.

The bottom line was that I was in big trouble. The window slammed shut. The coyotes had gained a few steps on me and I was beginning to feel the strain and exhaustion of the chase. Didn't coyotes ever get tired? Maybe not, but I was starting to wear down.

Things were looking pretty grim, fellers. I was

gasping for breath and I could hear the brothers behind me, laughing and chuckling and muttering threats about all the things they would do when they caught me.

I had one last trick in my bag of tricks. Over my shoulder, I yelled, "Hey Snort . . . HA!" Would it work one last time? I held my breath and waited.

Snort yelled back, "Ha your own self! Rip and Snort not fall for dummy Ha-Ha Game one more time in a row, ho ho!"

Well, that did it. I was out of luck, out of time, and out of breath. My cook was goosed.

# CHAPTER ELEVEN

# Trapped in
# Sally May's House!

**B**ut then something happened, something pretty amazing, something I hadn't counted on. As I was rounding the southwest corner of the house on Lap #6, I heard the voice of an angel.

"Hankie, over here! I've got the scween off the window. Huwwy and jump into my woom!"

Who? What?

Holy smokes, it was Little Alfred, calling to me from his bedroom window! He had managed to unhook the screen and set it on the ground, and now the window was open and waiting for me to dive in.

I altered course and took dead aim for the . . . you know, it was awfully dark out there, and to tell you the truth, I was having a hard time seeing the open window. Okay, we would have to do this on instruments.

I turned to the massive computer screen of my mind and began typing in the various codes and commands that would activate the program. Data Control clicked and whirred, then came the message: *"Wednesday's Special: cornbread and beans."*

Cornbread and beans! What kind of . . .

Okay, we had gotten a garbage message from Data Control, so this would have to be a seat-of-the-pants penetration of the window. I lined everything up, made one last check of the position of the North Star, and hit the Launch Button.

"Charge, bonzai! Make way, fellers, I'm coming through!"

BONK!

Okay, somebody had moved the window. No kidding. I had everything lined up, see, and we're talking crosshairs right on the center of the open window, but hey, what can you do when they start moving windows? I had done all a dog could do, and you probably think that I fell back to the ground and was devoured by the cannibal brothers.

Nope. At the last possible second, Little Alfred grabbed my left hind leg and hung on. He wasn't stout enough to pull me through the window, but he hung on and gave me just enough time to twist

around, snag the windowsill with my front paws, and haul myself up and into the house.

Whew! Boy, that had been too close for comfort.

Now that I was safe inside, Little Alfred leaned out the window and—you'll be impressed by this, I sure was—he leaned out the window and *spit* at the coyotes. No kidding. What a fine lad! What a little hero!

And then he yelled, "Go away and weeve my doggie awone!"

I guess nobody had ever spit . . . spat . . . sput . . . had ever sput on them before. Sputted. They were so shocked and amazed, they turned and slinked . . . slank . . . slunk . . .

I guess nobody had ever done that to them, so they turned to leave.

On seeing this, I felt a surge of new energy and courage. I rushed to the window and gave them one last burst of righteous indignature. "That's right, walk away! What a couple of losers you turned out to be. One more minute and I would have given you bums the thrashing you so richly deserved, and if you ever come back into my yard, by George, I'll do it. And I'm not kidding!"

Pretty impressive, huh? You bet. Why, if Alfred hadn't caught me and held me back, there's no telling what might have happened. Heck, I might very well have gone back out there and stomped a mudhole in their faces. I was *that* mad. Really.

But it was probably a good thing that the boy held me back, before my righteous anger spilled over and caused terrible damage to the property. Just imagine the scene the next morning when Sally May went outside: coyote blood all over her grass and flowers, arms and legs and ears hanging from the trees . . .

Anyway, he managed to hold me back until I got control of my terrible rage, and then I sent the fleabag coyotes on their way with one last stinging reply. "And what's more, your momma wears overshoes!"

Oops. Maybe I should have . . . they . . . well, they turned around and . . . uh . . . came back, shall we say, and now they really looked hot. Little Alfred glanced at me and I glanced at him. He said, "Maybe you shouldn't have barked at them, Hankie."

Right. I had made . . . that is, a mistake had probably been made. Poor judgment had probably been used. The situation should have been, uh, left alone. But let me hasten to add that this was very abnormal behavior for coyotes, because . . . well, they just never did this kind of thing. They never, ever came up into yards or hung around houses.

So, in a sense, we might say . . . okay, I messed up, and there they were, standing under our window again. "What Hunk say about coyote momma?"

I swallowed hard and eased my face to the window ledge. "Hey, Snort, how's it going? I thought you guys . . ."

"What Hunk say about coyote momma? Better have good story this time, or maybe Rip and Snort jump through window too, ho ho."

I turned to Little Alfred. Through wags and worried looks and other communication media, I beamed him an urgent message. "Son, I think you'd better close that window, because if you don't, it's liable to start leaking coyotes."

He nodded and reached up for the window. He grabbed it with both hands and pulled down. It didn't move. He pulled again. It didn't move. It was one of those old wood-framed windows, don't you see, and sometimes they get warped.

The boy whispered, "I can't get it cwosed."

I took a deep gulp of air and poked my head outside. "Okay, guys, we've been talking this over in here, and we've decided to issue an apology. It seems that a tasteless and cruel remark was made about your mother, and tonight, right here in front of everyone, we're going to issue a retraction. That tasteless remark should never have been made and we're going to correct the record to read, 'Your mother, your sweet and saintly mother, never ever wore overshoes—not the five-buckle variety or even the pull-over kind.' What do you say?"

The brothers traded smirks. "Coyote momma not so sweet or saintingly. Coyote momma mean old bag."

"Okay, no problem. We'll put that into the record. 'Your momma, who is a mean old bag, never ever wore overshoes of any kind.' How does that sound?"

They held a whispering conference. "Sound okay, but Rip and Snort still berry mad about Potty Chicken and stupid Ha-Ha Game, and maybe sit here under window and wait for Hunk to come out, ho ho."

The boy and I moved away from the window. We felt some relief that the brothers weren't going to attack the house, but it still left us with a small problem: how were Drover and I going to . . .

*Drover!* Holy smokes, Little Drover was still out there in the darkness, perhaps hiding behind some bush or shrubbery, and we know about coyotes and their powerful sense of smell, right? They can track down an ant in a five-section pasture. They would find Drover and . . .

The poor little mutt! I rushed to the window and . . . yipes, there they were, Rip and Snort, so I, uh, backed away and called, "Drover! Drover! Run for your life, son, the coyotes are still in the yard!"

In the silence of the night, I heard his faint reply. "Help! Help!"

My heart raced. My eyes darted from side to side. Did I dare go back out there and launch a suicidal rescue mission to find the poor little guy? Uh . . . probably not, but before I had to make a solid commitment on that deal, I realized . . .

HUH?

I couldn't believe it. How had he . . . *He was already inside the house and hiding under Little Alfred's bed!*

I marched over to the bed and poked my nose underneath. "Drover, how did you get in here before I did?"

He gave me his patented silly grin. "Oh, hi. I just jumped through the window."

"And how many times do I have to tell you to hold the formation and wait for your leader to give the orders? I was out there circling the house. I could have been mauled by those mugs."

"Yeah, I was worried sick."

"Oh right, sure. Drover, sometimes I just . . . Come out from under that bed immediately." He wormed his way out. "I must warn you, this will go into my report. For running from the field of battle, you will get five Chicken Marks."

"Fine with me."

"What? Stop muttering."

"I said, oh, bug juice."

I gave him a glare of purest steel. "Bug juice? What is that supposed to mean?"

"Well, I wanted to say a naughty word but I knew I'd get a Chicken Mark, so I said . . . bug juice. I guess."

"Well, it goes down as naughty language. Now you're up to seven Chicken Marks. Get off the floor and pay attention. I'm sorry to inform you that we're not out of this deal yet. The coyotes have parked themselves right under the window. We're trapped in here and can't get out."

Drover grinned. "Yeah, but that's not a problem, 'cause we're inside the house, safe and sound."

I narrowed my eyes. "Drover, there's nothing safe about two dogs inside *this* house. Have you forgotten whose house this is?"

"Well, let's see. Little Alfred's?"

"No, wrong. It's Sally May's house, and what if . . ."

At that very moment—hang on, fellers, this gets scarier and scarier—at that very moment, my ears picked up a sound in the darkness. I lifted both ears

113

and focused. It appeared to be coming from . . . the other end of the house, in the general direction of . . .

Gulk.

It sounded a whole lot like the squeaking of a bed. And then the sound of feet, slippered feet swishing across the floor. The feet were . . . coming in our direction.

I whirled away from my nincompoop assistant and saw a look of frozen fear on Little Alfred's face. He'd heard it too, and he whispered, "Uh-oh. My mom's coming, and if she finds y'all dogs in here . . ."

He didn't need to say any more. Suddenly my whole life passed before my very eyes. Suddenly I realized that after a long and glorious career as Head of Ranch Security, my life had come down to this—a choice between diving through the open window and taking my chances with the cannibal brothers, or staying in the house and facing Sally May in one of her Thermonuclear Moments.

Gulp.

I couldn't even imagine what she would say or do if she caught us in the house. I mean, this had happened a time or two before, us getting caught in the house, and I seemed to remember that Sally May's last words on the subject had been, *"If this ever happens again . . ."*

My mouth was terribly dry. I shot a glance at the

open window. Was there a chance that the Ha-Ha Game might work one last time? I mean, it had saved our hides several times that evening and maybe . . . no, the brothers had figured it out. Leaping out the window would be sure and sudden . . .

The footsteps were in the kitchen now, coming our way. I could almost see her face—her eyes wide and wild and flaming, coils of smoke pouring out of her nostrils, her teeth transformed into . . . into vampire teeth and . . .

I rushed to the computer screen of my mind and typed in a desperate message: *"Red Alert Emergency! Clear the lines! What the heck do we do now?"*

The message from Data Control came back in a flash: *"Highway construction next seven miles. All boots ten percent off. Get rid of those ugly blemishes with turkey oil. System failure. Blub."*

We were doomed. Data Control had failed us in our hour of greatest need.

# CHAPTER TWELVE

# A Huge
# Moral Victory

I turned a pair of tragic eyes toward my little pal. For a moment, it appeared that he was frozen by fear and couldn't speak. Then he whispered, "Get under the bed and hide!"

We didn't need to be told twice. In a flash, Drover and I scrambled ourselves underneath the bed. There we held our respective breaths and listened to the pounding of our respective hearts— and to the footsteps that were coming closer and closer.

The door opened with an eerie squeak. The light came on. Through the opening between the floor and the bed, I could see a pair of feet—feet wearing pink slippers. They belonged to . . . gulp . . . Sally May.

Then came the voice, the dreaded voice, the voice that struck fear in the hearts of all dogs and little boys. "Alfred Leroy, what are you doing up at this hour of the night, and why is your window open?"

There was a long moment of silence. In that long terrible moment of silence, I found myself . . . well, I noticed that her feet and ankles were right there, only inches away from the end of my nose, and I know it sounds crazy, but all at once I felt this desire, this overpowering desire to . . . well, lick her on the ankle.

It was crazy. I knew it was crazy, but sometimes we dogs get these . . . these powerful urges to do crazy things, and . . . and sometimes we can control them and sometimes we can't. This time . . .

Before I could get control of these impulses, my tongue shot out and . . . luff wuff muff . . . holy smokes, just as my tongue had reached out to the fully extended position, she took a step toward the window . . . *and stepped on it!* On my tongue, not on the window. She stepped on my tongue.

And suddenly ten thousand pounds of tongue-crushing pressure pressed down on my tongue. My eyes bulged out. Waves of pain raced up through my mouth, down my spinebone, and out to the end of my tail. I let out a screech of pain but . . . well, noth-

ing came out. I mean, you can't screech when someone's standing on your tongue. Try it sometime.

Actually, it was lucky for me that I couldn't
screech, for a moment later she removed her foot
and continued her walk to the window. "Alfred,
why is your window open? What are you doing?"

I realized that Drover was giving me a loony
stare, so I whispered, "See tepped on my pung. I
hope it not boken."

"No thanks, I'm stuffed."

I stared in to the vacuum of his eyes for a
moment, trying to fit his words into some kind of
pattern. But other things were happening and I
didn't have time to . . .

Little Alfred said, "Mom, some coyotes came up into the yard and they're sitting wight under my window."

Silence fell over the room. "Alfred, honey, coyotes don't come that close to the house. Surely it's the dogs, and if they're in my yard . . ."

"No, Mom, they're coyotes, honest. Come wook."

Her feetsteps moved to the window. I heard a loud gasp. "Oh my stars, they are coyotes! Loper, come here and hurry! We've got . . ."

He was already there, Loper was. I could see his bare feet on the floor, only inches away from my . . . I know it sounds crazy, but all at once . . .

NO! I refused to yield to any more foolish impulses. Instead, I turned to Drover and whispered, "Let's get out of here!"

"You know, Hank, I don't think that's such a good . . ."

I didn't have time to argue. See, it had suddenly occurred to me that both Loper and Sally May were now in Alfred's room, right? So that meant that the coats were clear for us to make a run out of there. The coast was clear, shall we say.

I waited until Loper moved toward the window, and then, as quietly as a slithering snake, I eased my freight out of Alfred's bedroom and set sail for . . . I didn't know where. Anywhere. But as I was making my way through the kitchen, I suddenly realized (1) Drover, the little weenie, had disobeyed a direct order and had stayed under the bed; and (2) something in that kitchen smelled . . .

WOW! What was that? The aroma seemed to be coming from a spot near the sink, up on the counter. *Sniff, sniff.* Okay, you won't believe this. It was STEAK, waves of steakness, and all at once the pieces of the puddle began falling into place.

Don't you get it? Sally May had left the evening's steak scraps sitting on a plate on the counter and . . . do you see how this was all fitting together? The evening had begun several hours before with me . . . that is, with Pete trying to steal a luscious T-bone steak, and now the Wheel of Life had come full circle and had presented me with an opportunity, a rare opportunity, to . . .

*This was meant to be.* Those scraps had been left there for a purpose. I was there and the scraps were there, and this had to be more than a mere coincidence. I mean, a guy can't fight against the power of the ocean or the roar of a storm or the mysterious workings of Fate. Life has a way of fulfilling its own plan, right? And who was I to resist the workings of . . .

I, uh, hopped my front paws up onto the counter and peeked over the top. There it sat—a plate full of the most bodacious steak bones and steak fat I had ever seen. Yes, it was all coming clear now. I had been denied the Fabled Treasure of the Potted Chicken and here was my reward. *It was meant to be.* I eased my nose toward . . .

I heard voices coming from the bedroom.

LOPER: "Hyah, coyotes, hyah! Get on out of here, before I go for my shotgun!"

ALFRED: "There they go. Thanks, Dad."

SALLY MAY: "I sure hope they don't come back. Now, Alfred, let's all go back to bed and get some sleep."

ALFRED: "Dad, can you weeve my window open? My woom's kind of hot."

LOPER: "Well . . . all right, just this once, but we need to put that screen back on in the morning. I wonder how it came off."

ALFRED: "Oh . . . I guess the wind bwowed it . . . or somepin."

LOPER: "Hmmm. Well, sweet dreams."

I had pulled myself halfway up the counter, just far enough so that my tongue had reached the Fabled Treasure of the Steak Scraps (it wasn't broken after all, my tongue) and the wonderful taste of steakness was beginning to tingle its way down . . .

Someone was coming! Could I bear to give it up, this plate of . . . Yes, I had to run for my life. I eased myself down to the floor and . . . Where could I go? I really hadn't given that much, uh, thought, to be honest, and all at once . . .

The utility room. Nobody would go out to the utility room in the middle of the night, would they? Heck no. I mean, the utility room was for washing clothes and pulling off dirty boots and stuff like that, and yes, it would be the safest place in the house.

I went to Full Flames on all engines, spun my paws on the slick limoleun floor, and flew into the darkness of the utility room. There was just enough light coming from the kitchen so that I could see a pile of dirty sheets lying on the floor in front of the washing machine. Hey, that was the place for me! I nosed my way under the sheets and then went straight into a program we call Nobody's Here.

I shut down all breathing mechanisms, lay as still as a log, and waited for them to go back to . . . footsteps? Footsteps coming into the utility room? That was impossible, outrageous! Why would any-one go out into the utility room in the middle of the . . .

The footsteps came closer and closer. They stopped right beside me. Had I been discovered? I held my breath and waited. Then the silence, the terrible silence, was fractured by a man's voice.

"Boy, something sure stinks in here."

It was Loper. At that point, I dared to peek one eye out of a fold in the sheets. There he stood, towering above me like a . . . something. A huge scowling tree. He sampled the air with his nose and shook his head.

He yawned and started toward the door into the kitchen. So far, so good. But then . . . he tripped over the pile of laundry, the very pile of laundry in which I was hiding, and in the process, he stepped on my tail!

Oh pain! Oh hurt! A burning jolt of electrical pain went ripping up my tail section, and for a moment I thought I would yelp. I mean, that's what most dogs do when their tails get stepped on, right? It's a perfectly natural, healthy reaction to the indignity and so forth of being trampled, but this time . . . no, I couldn't allow myself to yelp or squall or make any sound at all.

I had to maintain strict radio silence. And you know what? I did. Yes, my eyes bulged out. Yes, my ears flew straight up. Yes, a yelp tried to form itself in the deep throatalary region of my throat, but somehow I managed to keep a lid on it.

Loper stumbled a few steps, then caught himself. He turned a glare toward the pile of . . . well, the pile of ME and the sheets, is what it was, and

I heard him mutter, "What the heck was that?" He bent at the waist and reached a hand toward the sheet.

My heart was pounding in my ears. I focused all my powers on concentration and tried to flatten myself into a . . . into *an invisible pancake,* a pancake so thin that it would be undetectable by human eyes. Could I do it?

Heck no, but what else can a guy think about when he's out of luck and about to be exposed for all the world to see? He thinks about becoming . . . well, an invisible pancake.

I felt his fingers on the sheet. Then . . .

You probably think he jerked away the sheet and there I lay, a quivering puddle of dog hair. Not so fast. You forgot about Little Alfred, right? Well, all at once the boy appeared in the doorway and said, "Hey Dad, can you tuck me into bed? I'm scared of the dark."

The fingers remained on the sheet, and Loper said, "There's something in this pile of laundry."

"I'm awful sweepy, Dad. Pweese tuck me in? And thanks for wunning off the coyotes. I was scared."

Two seconds crawled past. Three seconds. I hadn't taken a decent breath of air in five minutes and was about to smother. Loper sighed. "All right, son. Let's tuck you into bed."

His footsteps left the room and I dared to grab a breath of air.

He tucked Little Alfred into bed and said good night. He walked out of the boy's bedroom and yawned, then his eyes turned to the utility room. He took a step in my direction. And stopped. "Oh well." He turned off the kitchen light and shuffled off to his bedroom.

I almost fainted with relief! I waited for five minutes, until I could hear nothing but the rumble of Loper's snoring, then tiptoed out of the utility room and headed for the . . . *sniff, sniff* . . . headed straight for the kitchen counter. I mean, things that are *meant to be* should never be ignored, right? And that plate of steak scraps had been left there for a purpose—a Higher Purpose that would wrap up all the loose ends in the case and bring a flood of new meaning into my life.

I, uh, hopped up on my back legs and reached my paws over the kitchen counter. The fragrant waves of steakness filled my nostrils, bringing a rush of meaning and purpose into the darkness of my . . .

HUH?

Someone was behind me, and he clamped me with his arms.

You thought it was Loper or Sally May, right?

"No, no, Hankie. Weeve the scwaps awone. You have to go now."

Whew! It was Little Alfred, my greatest pal and hero, and he probably thought . . . hey, I was ready to leave the house, no kidding, but about those scraps . . .

He reached up and snagged a gorgeous T-bone and held it in front of my nose. "I'll wet you have it when you jump out the window."

Hey, that would work! You bet, no problem. You see how these things sort themselves out? When things are *meant to be,* they just naturally find their own solution.

I followed the boy into the bedroom and whispered to the runt. "All right, Drover, you can come out now. I've secured the house and our mission is completed. And you'll be happy to know that I've just been chosen to receive the Golden Bone Award."

He came wiggling out from under the bed. "Oh good, and maybe I'll get one too."

"Forget that, pal. You'll get just what you deserve—a big nothing."

"Oh, bug juice."

I was about to give the dunce another Chicken Mark when . . . hmm, Little Alfred pitched the bone out the window, and all at once it was time for the

Closing Ceremonies. I gave him a juicy lick on the cheek and he gave me a hug. It was a pretty touching ceremony, I mean, the boy and I had gone through a real . . . but I had a bone waiting for me, so I cut it short and crept out the . . .

I couldn't believe my eyes! The cat had come out of nowhere and was in the process of eating and slobbering all over my Golden Bone Award! For a second or two, my mind went blank and I saw nothing but a huge curtain of red. This was IT. I couldn't stand any more. Right there in the yard, I would pulverize the cat for all the . . . the list was long. Trying to steal my evidentiary material, telling me the big whopperous lie about the Potted Chicken (which I had never believed, no kidding), and now, slobbering on my Golden Bone Award.

But at the last second, I caught myself. Instead of giving the little snot the pounding he so richly deserved, I would defeat him through cunning and strategy and higher intelligence.

Heh heh. You'll be impressed by this. See, instead of yielding to my savage instincts, and waking up the house again and getting flogged by Sally May's broom, I lured the foolish cat into my most secret and deadly ploy—the Ha-Ha Game.

Ha ha ha ha ha . . . okay, maybe he . . . ha ha ha ha ha . . . the stupid cat . . . ha ha ha ha . . .

Skip it. Once again, I had won a, uh, huge moral victory over the imbecile cat and had brought the ranch through another dark and dangerous night. Around here, we consider that a pretty good piece of ranch work.

Case . . . ha ha ha ha ha ha . . . closed . . . ha ha ha ha ha . . .

# What's in store for Hank the Cowdog?

In his next adventure, the Head of Ranch Security goes out on the town with Dog-pound Ralph. Hank finds himself trapped on a cattle truck, arrested on false charges, and stranded up a tree with a bunch of hungry buzzards. Can he clear his name and make it back to the ranch in one piece? Turn the page for a sample of what's next for Hank in *Hank the Cowdog #38: The Fling*.

# Escape from the Dogcatcher's Truck

I waited for Ralph to do his thinking. I figured he would be pretty slow at it, and he was. Ralph didn't get in much of a hurry for anything.

He yawned and stretched and walked around the cage, looking out. "It's kind of a warm day, ain't it?"

"Yes. It's warm and very depressing."

"Uh-huh. Days are like that sometimes."

"I suppose."

"It's getting close to fall, ain't it?"

"Uh, Ralph, I don't want to rush you . . ."

"I've always liked the fall."

"You were going to think about my problem, remember?"

"Don't rush me."

1

"Sorry."

Again, I waited. Ralph sat down and scratched his right ear. "Wax."

"I beg your pardon?"

He stared at me. "Wax. I get wax in my ears and it tickles sometimes."

"How interesting. So then you have to scratch, I suppose."

"Yalp. Sometimes it helps and sometimes it don't."

"Mmmm, yes." I watched as he kicked himself in the ear. "It's probably better by now."

"Nope, still tickles."

"Great." Seconds crawled by. I watched him scratch and tried to contain myself. The pickup lurched to a stop. "Uh-oh. Is this the dog pound?"

Ralph glanced around. "Nope. Coffee time. Jimmy Joe'll be here for thirty minutes. We do this every day."

Sure enough, we had pulled up in front of the Dixie Dog Cafe. The dogcatcher climbed out, stretched a kink out of his back, and went inside. My gaze drifted back to Ralph. He was still scratching his ear.

Ralph was scratching, not the dogcatcher.

"Uh, Ralph, I've always been a dog of few words."

"Good."

"But under the circumstances, I think I'll depart from tradition."

"You worry too much."

"Could we discuss my future? You said something about developing a plan, or words to that effect."

"Uh-huh. Already did."

"You already..." I stared at him. "You've already got a plan in mind?"

"Yup. A good one too."

"Ralph, I'd be the last dog in the world to doubt what you say, but I've been here in this prison cage for the last half hour and I've seen no evidence that you were thinking or planning. You've been scratching, if I may be so blunt."

He grinned. "Helps me think, scratching does."

"Good. Fine. Could we discuss your thoughts? I mean, I don't want to seem impatient or doubtful or pushy..."

He raised a paw to his lips. "Shhhh. You're starting to get on my nerves."

That was more than I could take. "I'm starting to get on your nerves? I'm sorry, pal, but shall we be frank and earnest?"

"I'm Ralph, Dogpound Ralph, and I think your name's Hank."

"I know your name and I know my name, and you know what else? You're starting to get on MY nerves. My life is at stake here and I demand that you stop noodling around and get down to business."

"You do, huh?"

"Yes, I most certainly do."

He yawned, pushed himself up, and waddled over to the cage door. He gave it a push with his left front paw and ... you won't believe this ... it swung open!

My eyes darted from the door to Ralph and back to the door. "How'd you do that?"

"Gave it a shove."

"I saw that part, but how'd you know it wasn't latched? I mean, I never would have thought ..."

"That's the problem, see. You talk all the time and don't do much thinking."

"I resent that. For your information, I don't talk all the time."

"What are you doing now?"

"I'm ... how'd you know the door wasn't latched?"

"'Cause I pay attention. 'Cause I knew Jimmy Joe didn't lock it. You want to leave or stay?"

My gaze went to the open door. "This isn't a trick, is it? I mean, this seems too easy, Ralph, and somehow I smell a rat."

He heaved a sigh. "The door's open."

4

"Right, but consider this, Ralph. My background is in Security Work, and we're trained never to fall for the obvious. When something seems too good to be true . . . hey, where are you going?"

He hopped out of the cage and trotted away.

I edged toward the door and did a rapid Sniff and Check. See, I still wasn't convinced that this wasn't some kind of setup deal, and I wanted to check it out for, well, electronic sensor devices, powerful energy fields, magnetic thermocouples, and the other devices that might have been installed on the door.

To my surprise, it was clean. Nothing.

I dived through the door and into Sweet Freedom, hurried away from the awful prison truck where I had been confined for weeks, and caught up with Ralph. He was walking down the middle of a side street. I fell in step beside him. For a minute or two, neither of us spoke.

"Ralph, one question. If you knew that door was unlatched, why didn't you say so?"

"Too much trouble."

"What? I thought my life was about to end, and it was too much trouble to for you to tell me otherwise?"

"You're still alive, ain't you?"

"I'm still alive, but I aged several years."

"Aged beats dead."

"I won't argue that, Ralph, but . . . where are we going?"

He stopped and sat down in the middle of the street. He looked at me with his big sad eyes. "You just keep firing questions, don't you?"

"Asking questions is part of my job, Ralph. I ask questions, seek answers, and follow every clue to its . . . where are we going?"

"I don't know where you're going, but I'm out on a fling."

"Oh? What's a fling?" I heard him heave a sigh. "Sorry, but I'm from the country. I don't know what a fling is."

"A fling's a fling."

"Great. So what is it?"

It took me a long time, but finally I managed to drag an explanation out of him. Here's what he told me.

He lived at the dog pound, remember? Only he wasn't one of the convict dogs. He was Jimmy Joe Dogcatcher's pet. Once every month or two, he got tired of living behind bars and went on a "fling," which meant that for several hours or days, he indulged himself in naughty behavior and played chase games with Jimmy Joe.

I found this strange. "Wait a minute. The dog-

6

catcher lets you do this? He's part of the game?"

"Yup. We both get tired of the same old stuff. When business is slow, Jimmy Joe forgets to lock the door."

At that very moment, a car approached us from the west, and there we were, sitting in the middle of the street. The car screeched its brakes, swerved, honked, and zipped past us. The breeze from the car caused my ears to ripple.

"Hey, Ralph, maybe we ought to get out of the middle of the street, huh?"

He grinned. "Naw. They'll swerve. They always do."

"Yeah, but what if they don't? What if . . . Wait a minute. Is this part of your fling?"

"Uh-huh. Kind of exciting, ain't it?"

"Well, I . . . I've never thought about that, Ralph, but to be real honest . . ."

Another car came along, this one from the other direction. The driver didn't see us until the last second. He hit his brakes, smoked his tires on the pavement, and brought the car to a stop just inches away from us.

Ralph's eyes brightened with . . . I don't know what. Some kind of devilish delight, I suppose, and though I had known Ralph for quite a while, I'd never seen this side of him before.

He chuckled and gave me a wink. "That was a good 'un, wasn't it?"

The driver stuck his head out the window and blew his horn. "Get out of the road, you idiots! What do you think this is, a parking lot for mutts? I'm calling the dogcatcher!"

With that, he roared away, leaving us to roast in his angry glare.

I turned back to Ralph. "That guy was pretty mad."

"Yeah, it drives 'em nuts, me sitting in the middle of the road."

"And you think this is fun, right?"

"Yup. And you know what else?"

I cast glances over my shoulders, just in case another car was coming. "No, I don't know what else. What else?"

His eyes, usually so sad and dull, were sparkling. "There's funner stuff yet to come. The Fling has started. Jimmy Joe'll be after us any minute now."

I moved myself out of the road and sat down on the curb. "In that case, I'll be leaving soon. To be perfectly honest, I think this is a little ... weird." Another car zoomed past, missing Ralph by inches. "Ralph, you're going to get smashed. What's the point of all this?"

He joined me at the curb, his ears dragging the

ground and his toenails clicking on the pavement. "The point is that I get tired of being a good dog, so I bust out and do naughty things. Don't you ever wish you could be naughty?"

"No. I guess we're different, Ralph. You're just a jailhouse mutt. Me, I'm Head of Ranch Security."

"Uh-huh."

"It's a very heavy responsibility."

"Yalp. So you don't want to go with me and be naughty?"

"Of course not, and I'm shocked you'd even suggest it."

"Oh. Well, see you around." He walked away.

"Good-bye, Ralph. I'll be heading back to the ranch. I appreciate your help and so forth, but I want the record to show . . . " He kept walking and I had to yell. "Ralph, I want the record to state that I don't approve of this dark side of your . . . What sort of naughtiness did you have in mind?"

"I'm gonna eat me a steak."

Huh?

At this point, we must bring this story to a close. What follows has been sealed and classified Top Secret. It won't be available to the general public for twenty-five years.

Sorry.

# Have you read all of Hank's adventures?